MW00850374

Graveyard Dog

Also From Darynda Jones

CHARLEY DAVIDSON SERIES

First Grave on the Right
For I have Sinned: A Charley Short Story
Second Grave on the Left
Third Grave Dead Ahead
Fourth Grave Beneath my Feet
Fifth Grave Past the Light
Sixth Grave on the Edge
Seventh Grave and No Body
Eight Grave After Dark
Brighter than the Sun: A Reyes Novella
The Dirt on Ninth Grave
The Curse of Tenth Grave
Eleventh Grave in Moonlight
The Trouble with Twelfth Grave
Summoned to Thirteenth Grave
The Graveyard Shift: A Charley Novella
The Gravedigger's Son: A Charley Novella
The Graveside Bar and Grill: A Charley Novella
The Grave Robber: A Charley Novella

BETWIXT & BETWEEN

Betwixt
Bewitched
Beguiled
Moonlight and Magic

THE NEVERNEATH

A Lovely Drop
The Monster

MYSTERY

SUNSHINE VICRAM SERIES

A Bad Day for Sunshine

A Good Day for Chardonnay
A Hard Day for a Hangover

YOUNG ADULT

DARKLIGHT SERIES
Death and the Girl Next Door
Death, Doom, and Detention
Death and the Girl He Loves

Graveyard Dog

A Charley Davidson Novella

By Darynda Jones

1001 DARK NIGHTS
PRESS

Graveyard Dog
A Charley Davidson Novella
By Darynda Jones

1001 Dark Nights

ISBN: 979-8-88542-072-3

Published by 1001 Dark Nights Press, an imprint of Evil Eye Concepts, Incorporated

Acknowledgments from the Author

I just want to thank everyone at 1001 Dark Nights. I'm so in love with all of you!

Thank you, Chelle and Liz, for all the last-minute edits. I know, right? It's so unlike me!

And thank YOU, Grimlet, for staying by Charley and the gang's side. I loved writing Michael's story so much, and we have a new member (or two) for the team. So much more wonderful on the way, so stay tuned!

XOX,
Darynda

One Thousand and One Dark Nights

Once upon a time, in the future…

I was a student fascinated with stories and learning. I studied philosophy, poetry, history, the occult, and the art and science of love and magic. I had a vast library at my father's home and collected thousands of volumes of fantastic tales.

I learned all about ancient races and bygone times. About myths and legends and dreams of all people through the millennium. And the more I read the stronger my imagination grew until I discovered that I was able to travel into the stories... to actually become part of them.

I wish I could say that I listened to my teacher and respected my gift, as I ought to have. If I had, I would not be telling you this tale now.
But I was foolhardy and confused, showing off with bravery.

One afternoon, curious about the myth of the Arabian Nights, I traveled back to ancient Persia to see for myself if it was true that every day Shahryar (Persian: شهریار*, "king") married a new virgin, and then sent yesterday's wife to be beheaded. It was written and I had read that by the time he met Scheherazade, the vizier's daughter, he'd killed one thousand women.*

Something went wrong with my efforts. I arrived in the midst of the story and somehow exchanged places with Scheherazade – a phenomena that had never occurred before and that still to this day, I cannot explain.

Now I am trapped in that ancient past. I have taken on Scheherazade's life and the only way I can protect myself and stay alive is to do what she did to protect herself and stay alive.

Every night the King calls for me and listens as I spin tales. And when the evening ends and dawn breaks, I stop at a point that leaves him breathless and yearning for more. And so the King spares my life for one more day, so that he might hear the rest of my dark tale.

As soon as I finish a story... I begin a new one... like the one that you, dear reader, have before you now.

Chapter One

No good deed goes unpunished.
—Oscar Wilde

Michael Cavalcante tried to remember the exact circumstances that'd led to his sudden and alarming inability to see straight. Or to unlock his throbbing jaw. Or to hear anything other than a high-pitched ringing in his ears. Either he could now perceive frequencies otherwise reserved for dogs, or he'd been ambushed by a tiny brunette with a frying pan and trust issues.

The bad news: If he died, it would take weeks for anyone to find him. He'd just settled in for the night and caught a nice buzz when the call came in, so he'd left his bike at home and taken an Uber. No one knew where he'd gone. Would anyone wonder why he'd disappeared? Would they worry about his fragile well-being? Not likely since there was nothing fragile about him. But a guy could dream.

The good news: Death would be preferable to the throbbing in his jaw. And his neck. And his right shoulder. Actually, anything would be preferable. Fire ants. Torture. An IRS audit.

He lifted his lids long enough to realize the sun had crested the horizon, the light a soft glow around him. He'd been out a while.

The sound of metal scraping against wood broke through the ringing in his ears, followed by the soft rustling of feet and a cascade of falling objects like a box being dumped out beside him. He tried again to focus on his surroundings and received a stabbing pain along his left temple for his efforts, so he gave up.

He let his lids drift shut and leaned his head back against the cool, smooth surface of what he could only assume was an oven door. Or possibly a dishwasher. Either way, his hands had been bound with a rope to the handle of whichever kitchen appliance his captor felt would hold him best.

They didn't know him very well.

It was this complex. The apartment complex he'd been conned into buying by a fourteen-going-on-forty-year-old named Elwyn Alexandra Loehr. The preternatural daughter of two gods, Elwyn had been making strange requests of the entire team commissioned to protect her.

She'd had his friend Donovan start following the team's gorgeous, ask-no-questions doctor—a godsend, considering their lifestyles—only to find out the woman was a wraith from another dimension. She'd encouraged another member, Eric, to take a break and visit his old friend in Idaho, where he stopped a woman from being killed by a man who'd been stalking her for years. And she'd convinced Michael to invest in real estate. To make something of himself. To expand his horizons. As if watching over the girl destined to save the world from a demon uprising wasn't enough.

He hadn't questioned her motives then, but he was beginning to now. She was far too intelligent for her own good, and he was beginning to see a pattern, as though she were moving pieces on a chessboard. Collecting a pool of humans with supernatural abilities. Gathering her army.

The whole thing made him nervous. At this point in her life, she was far too young to face an opponent like the king of Hell. She needed time, and they needed to come up with a plan. Together.

Besides, Michael didn't have a supernatural bone in his body. He probably would've known to steer clear of this building if he did. Strange things had been happening since he bought it. Like lights flashing at all hours of the night. And creepy sounds keeping the tenants awake. Clearly, it was cursed. Or haunted. Or both.

Probably both.

He made a mental note to call in a favor from Elwyn's mother and have the place exorcized. What were friends for, if not to purge one's demons? Then again, would the building still be standing when she finished? She'd exorcized a nasty bottom dweller out of one of his best friends a few years back, and he'd turned out okay—if one used a *very* loose definition of the word.

A lyrical voice wafted toward him, one with a soft British accent. "Excuse me, my lord, would you like milk and sugar?"

The situation just got a whole lot weirder.

He pried open his right, less traumatized eye. A little girl, who couldn't have been more than five, sat cross-legged on the floor in front of him. She sat in the middle of a thousand tiny plastic dishes and held up a pink plastic teacup.

A bevy of wild, dark curls encircled her head, some wilder than others, as though she'd just woken up. She wore pink pajamas, the kind with feet, and a single barrette did its best to keep one of the more brazen curls out of her eyes. But that's not what surprised him the most. Well, besides the whole situation. The girl's eyes. They were huge and a silvery brown, like the fur on the coyote he'd spotted outside the compound one foggy morning.

"Tea ought to have milk at least, don't you think?" she asked, raising dark brows until her forehead wrinkled.

He wondered what part of England she was from and how she'd ended up living in Santa Fe, New Mexico.

She picked up a toy milk carton and poured it into his empty cup. "It's the civilized way to drink it, after all."

He grunted, and she glanced up at him as though surprised.

She put the cup down and picked up another plastic dish, just as empty as the first one. "One lump or two?" she asked as she held up what had to be her mother's tweezers.

He eyed her with a wariness usually reserved for psychopaths, scammers, and McDonald's employees. Was she punking him? Was this a joke? A setup? He wouldn't put it past his more asshole-inclined friends, but he had a killer headache and was starting to lose feeling in his hands. Surely, they wouldn't go this far. "I've had enough lumps for one day, thank you very much."

"As you wish." She pushed the cup toward him across the yellowing linoleum floor—the one he'd hated since he bought the place. It would be the first thing to go when he started the remodeling project. If he lived that long. These apartments were in serious need of an upgrade. Especially with the astronomical rent the tenants paid. Then again, this was Santa Fe.

A loud gasp came from the doorway, and a woman who looked eerily familiar rushed into the kitchen, snatched the girl to her, and backed away until they were both out of his reach. Which, at the moment, was like two inches, but she seemed determined to put space between them.

Then reality sank in. It was *her*. The woman who'd answered the door at two in the morning holding a frying pan. And possibly a Taser. Who did that?

"Oh, it's you," he said in his favorite language: sarcasm. "I didn't recognize you without the frying pan."

She had hair the same color as the girl's, hanging in soft waves around her face and past her shoulders. A similar bow-shaped mouth and eyes the same ashen brown confirmed their relationship.

"She's not my daughter," she said, frantically clutching the girl to her.

Or not.

"Mama," the girl pouted, placing the accent on the second *ma*, her lower lip jutting out.

"She's the neighbor's kid. They're British. I just watch her from time to time."

The girl tried to shake out of her grip. While she failed, she did manage to turn in the woman's arms and look up at her. "Why do you always say that?" she asked in her soft British accent—one the woman didn't have.

The laugh that escaped the older woman was so exaggerated and forced that Michael was appalled such talent had somehow eluded Hollywood scouts. She pulled the girl to her and petted her hair until he worried the child might go bald. "She's a bit dramatic."

The girl pushed at the brunette's hands. "Mama, stop."

"Look," Michael said, growing impatient. And numb. "Like I said when you answered the door this morning, I got a call about your heater."

"There's nothing wrong with my heater."

"Then why did you call?" he asked through gritted teeth.

"I didn't. But you know that already."

"I do?" He did? He was lost. Had he come to the wrong apartment? Damn it. How much had he drunk? He tried to count on his fingers but could no longer feel them.

The woman pushed the girl behind her as she walked closer to him. So close he could have easily taken her out with a single sweep of his leg and a triangle chokehold. And it wasn't like an oven—dishwasher?—door handle could hold him if he didn't want it to. Maybe for a few seconds. But he'd once fought a bear. Long story. He was fairly certain he could take an appliance door under the right circumstances.

Clearly not a criminal mastermind, the woman leaned close to him, the scent of peach shampoo washing over him, and said the oddest thing he'd heard all day. And he'd heard a lot of strange things already. "Be still."

He could barely move as it was. How much stiller could he get?

"You will forget the girl in sixty seconds."

"Mama!" the girl shouted in protest, tugging at the woman's robe—a micro-thin garment that did little to conceal the curves underneath.

How the fuck was he just now seeing them? The curves. It was the frying pan; it had to be. Because as she leaned even closer, her beautiful face came into focus, and he felt a rippling punch to his gut.

Unhinged and beautiful.

Just his type.

Son of a bitch.

"You will never remember her," she continued.

"Mama, don't," the girl said, her pout firmly in place. Only this time, she crossed her arms over her chest for added emphasis.

He leaned to the side to see her better. "I'm pretty sure I won't forget you anytime soon." He winked at her, and she giggled before a look of sadness shadowed her bright features.

"See?" she said, pointing at him. "He's light."

She would be pale, too, if she'd been hit with a frying pan and tied to a kitchen appliance.

The woman knelt and turned the girl toward her. "Get your go-bag, honey, and then lock yourself in my room."

Why would a five-year-old need a go-bag? He looked at the woman's profile, taking in the soft lines of her face and full mouth, and something reared up inside him. Something he didn't *want* rearing up. The desire to guard. Protect. Avenge.

"Who's after you?" he asked.

The woman jumped and turned to look at him, but just as quickly turned back to her daughter. "Hurry, sweetheart. We don't have much time."

The girl nodded obediently and rushed into a narrow hallway that led to the bedrooms. When she disappeared, the woman lifted her watch and waited.

"Can I change?" came a shout from one of the rooms.

"I've already grabbed you some clothes. They're on my bed."

"Okay," the girl said. She rushed out of her room carrying a backpack and entered the one across the hall, waving at Michael before closing and locking the door.

"Don't worry," the woman said, staring at her watch. "You won't remember me either."

He cocked his head to the side, trying to figure her out. "I don't know. You're pretty unforgettable."

She glanced at him, blinked several times, and then shouted, "Time!"

The girl didn't make a sound. How often had they practiced this scenario? And why?

He tried to rub his head, forgetting his wrists were bound. "Look, Killer, I'm all for bondage, but I may need a minute to get over this headache."

"Frying pans'll do that." She said it almost absently as she took some food out of a pantry and put it on the table.

He'd fought nature, animals, and gangs that would make a lesser man hightail it in the opposite direction. To be brought down by a forest sprite who weighed less than his saddlebags irked.

"You wouldn't happen to have any oxycodone, would you?"

She glared at him. "Why would I have that in my house?"

"Ibuprofen?" When she only glared at him, refusing to answer, he probed again. "Tylenol? Aspirin? Herbal tea?" Nothing. He rolled his eyes and winced, hoping the concussion killed him quickly. His deepest fear was suffering a lingering death. And spiders. Mostly spiders. "Can you at least answer one question?" he asked as she began transferring the food to a duffel bag. He realized almost all of it was either dry or canned. She knew what she was doing.

She ignored him as she worked around his form, and the plastic dishes sprawled across the floor, moving with the grace of a dancer. Then she looked up, clearly needing something above him. She bit her lip, trying to decide if the item was worth risking her life. She decided. He could see it in the determined set of her jaw. She knelt in front of him and locked those huge eyes onto his. "You will sit here for one hour, and then you will free yourself from the stove and leave."

His brows cinched together as he tried to figure out exactly how unhinged she was. A little worked for him on several levels, but pure madness? Not worth the hassle. He'd given it his all once. It'd ended badly.

"You will not move."

Damn it. She was inching her way up the loony scale with every word.

"You will not speak."

He was more of a thinker anyway.

"Once you cross the threshold, you will not remember me or what happened here."

He wouldn't forget her in a thousand lifetimes.

"You will go about your day as usual and never think of me again."

"Does this usually work?" he asked, genuinely curious.

Surprised, she jerked away from him, then repeated, "You will not speak."

"Right. I get that, but—"

"Stop talking," she said, her voice rising a notch with panic.

Fine. He'd play along. He closed his mouth and waited to see what she would do next. He wouldn't get anything out of her like this. She needed to trust him, but, apparently, he only had an hour to accomplish the feat. If that long.

She eyed him warily, then slowly went back to her task, glancing at him from over her shoulder every so often. After hauling the duffel bag off the table, she looked longingly once more at the cabinet above the stove. Whatever she wanted called to her. She stuck a nail between her teeth in thought, then leaned down to him again.

"Close your eyes and don't move," she said.

He obeyed. This was getting too interesting not to.

Then she stepped over him, one foot at his hip, the other between his legs. His muscles clenched in response. The scent of peaches drifted over him, and he lifted his lids—just barely—trying to see what she was up to. The robe parted at her knees as she reached up, and he caught a glimpse of her shapely thighs. He welded his teeth together when one of said thighs brushed his fingers.

She stepped back, and he remembered that he wasn't supposed to move, so he lowered his head again and sat there. Quiet. Bound. Obedient. This whole thing would've been much easier if he were a sub. He'd never been submissive a day in his life. He may have to rethink that.

After tossing the mystery item into the bag, she zipped it closed and then dragged it with both hands to the front door before hurrying back to her bedroom.

Michael sat there in thought for several long moments. She would never confide in him as long as he was tied up and unable to speak. No, he would have to convince her to open up to him. He just didn't know how.

Before he could decide, the bedroom door squeaked open, and the girl—now dressed in a pair of purple sweats and a hoodie—tiptoed out.

Michael closed his eyes again and waited as the girl crept past him to put her go-bag next to the duffel full of food. He watched her through heavily lidded eyes. She tiptoed to the refrigerator and took out a sparkly pink water bottle before stopping in front of him.

"Live well, my lord." She said the words a microsecond before she bent and placed a soft kiss on his cheek.

It broke him. He waited until she stepped back before moving. The shock on the girl's face when he looked up at her almost made him laugh, but he had to be quick. One jerk and the handle gave. He let it drop to the floor, then went to work on the ropes.

"Mommy!" the girl shouted, her British accent gone as she ran down the hall. "The prisoner escaped! The prisoner escaped!"

"That's impossible," the woman said, stepping into the hall as the girl ran past her into the room.

The knots in the rope weren't bad. Again, she knew what she was doing. But they took all of twenty seconds to discard.

The woman gasped, slammed the bedroom door, and locked it.

His boots plodded to the flimsy barrier. One shove, and he was in. Just in time to see the woman raise a gun and point it at his head.

Chapter Two

How soon after getting up
is it okay to take a nap?
—Meme

No. Not a gun. A black *toy* gun, the kind that shot foam darts. Seriously?

He crossed his arms and leaned against the doorframe, doing his best not to scare them and failing miserably.

The woman, now dressed in jeans and a long-sleeved V-neck, stood on the other side of the bed, holding the girl to her with one hand and the gun on him with the other.

"You're not fooling anyone with that piece of plastic, Killer."

The indignant expression that flashed across her face was almost worth the subsequent pain a chuckle evoked. Almost.

"How did you—?" She snapped her mouth shut, annoyance flitting across her face. No, not annoyance. Confusion. And fear. She drew in a shaky breath, doing her best to regroup, but the fear had taken hold. Though she kept her jaw firmly in place as she held onto what tattered remnants of defiance she could muster, the gun shook in her hand. Still, she was a fighter.

Attagirl.

He almost smiled, but he had genuinely scared the girl, and he was sorrier for that than anything.

"To the average person, this gun looks real," the woman said, holding it as still as she could while her gaze periodically darted around. Looking for a real weapon? A phone? An escape?

Michael did his best to seem innocuous, which was hard with his size.

And his features. A woman at a bar had once called him *The Hulk*. He didn't appreciate the comparison, but she wasn't wrong. "That looks about as real as those diamond rings you get from a gumball machine."

She raised her chin a visible notch. "You knowing the difference only confirms what I already suspected about you."

He cocked a single brow. "Yeah? What's that?"

"You're a criminal, through and through."

He shrugged. "I never said I wasn't."

The air left her lungs with his confession, and she inched toward a large, plate-glass window that led to the fire escape.

"How is he moving?" the girl asked.

For some reason, the woman kept the gun trained on him. If it made her feel safer, he was all for it. Her gaze darted to her dresser beside him for the third time, and he finally saw the Taser she'd electrocuted him with earlier. But it was closer to him than it was to her. Much closer.

He calculated how long it would take her to open the window and get her daughter and her outside. He would have more than enough time to intercept, but to what end? There were laws against holding someone against their will. And she could scream. He and cops didn't usually get along.

He held up both hands, doing his best to calm her. "Look, lady, I don't know who you are, but I got a call at two this morning about a heater on the fritz."

"It's not that cold. Why would someone call in the middle of the night?"

"Right?" he asked. Finally, validation. "I was asking myself that very thing."

She reached over and unlocked the window. "Even if you're telling the truth, I know the maintenance man very well. You're not him."

He ran a hand over his face. "He's with his wife, my property manager. They are both out having a baby."

She drew in a soft breath. "Allison is having her baby?"

"As we speak. And my maintenance tech is with her."

"Right," she said, the word drenched in disbelief as she tried to pry the window open. To no avail. "What's his name?"

"Steve McBride. He works for me. I own the building. You can call him and ask. My name is Michael."

Her gaze darted to the dresser again. Her phone sat right beside the Taser.

"Here." He picked up the cell and tossed it onto the bed, praying she wouldn't call the police. Hours spent at the station as he explained himself was all he needed.

The girl peeked out from behind her mother, wearing a grin that took up more real estate on her face than it had any right to. She wasn't scared. Was this like a game to her? He hoped so. No five-year-old should know the evils of men. Well, *other* men.

Relief flooded every cell in his body.

The woman reached for her phone just as his dinged with a text. He took it out of his back pocket. "It's a girl," he said, happy for the couple.

The brunette tapped three numbers, only three, and he knew his day was about to be even more ruined than it already was, but she paused before hitting the call button. "Let me see." She gestured toward his phone with her chin.

He tossed that to her, along with the Taser, hoping he wasn't making the biggest mistake of his life. But how else could he get her to trust him? To open up? Because he wanted to know who was after her. And why. And where he could find them.

She grabbed the Taser first and put it on the nightstand beside her, then his phone. After checking the messages, she slowly raised her eyes to his. "You're really the owner?"

He spread his hands. "I'm really the owner."

"I knew it!" the girl said, climbing up to sit on the bed. "I told you he was light. It's everywhere. He's like an angel."

He glared at her. That was going too far. Most angels were dicks.

She giggled.

Could the kid see auras? He'd certainly witnessed stranger things.

The woman tried to explain but couldn't figure out what to say. "I didn't—I-I thought—"

"Who's after you?" he asked, hoping for an answer this time.

"No one." When he offered her his best deadpan look, she added, "Someone from my past. When I saw you, I thought he'd found me."

"Why?" Before she could answer, he asked, "Is that window stuck?" That was a clear code violation. He'd been reading up on codes since he'd purchased the building.

When he walked around the bed toward them, the woman didn't grab the Taser. She grabbed the gun—the fake one—and pointed it at him. She really needed to up her game.

"Scoot," he said when he got close enough to be tased had she thought things through.

Instead, she kept the gun on him as she moved to the side.

"Ah, there are two latches. You only unlocked one." He unlatched the second and raised the window just to make sure it opened. It did, so he closed it, resecured the latches, and turned back to them. "Why did you think your ex had found you when you saw me?"

With every move slow and calculated, she inched around him, taking the girl with her as she backed toward the door.

He followed. Apparently, they were going to have this conversation in the kitchen. Or the living room that was as small as his left ventricle.

The minute they got to the kitchen, the woman rushed to the coffee maker and slammed a K-cup into the dispenser. Addiction was a terrible thing.

The girl waited for him to emerge from the hallway, then took his hand in hers and led him to the table. And…he was lost.

"Can you pick up your dishes, sweetheart?"

"Can't I just kick them to my room?"

The woman hid a smile and said sternly, "No, you may not."

"Mom," the girl said, drawing the title out until it formed several different-pitched syllables.

Michael pressed his lips together to keep an ill-mannered grin at bay. "Can I ask what your names are?" When the woman didn't answer, he added, "You know I can just look at your rental agreement."

She drew in a deep breath and turned to him. "I'm Izzy. That's Pickle."

"Pickle?" he asked, impressed.

"This week," Izzy added.

"Oh, yeah?" He smiled down at the girl as she tossed plastic dishes into a box that had seen better days. "What was it last week?"

"Biscuits and Gravy." Her face lit up like she'd just won a trophy.

He fought that grin again, tooth and nail. "I like it."

"Me, too, but Mommy said it was too long."

He chuckled. "I'm sensing a pattern. Are all your nicknames food-themed?"

She picked up a pink teapot with a cracked lid. "Yeah. I really like food."

"Get outta here. I do, too."

"Really?" She stood and plopped her crossed arms on the table. "What is your very favorite thing to eat?"

He thought for a moment, then said, "Probably biscuits and gravy with a pickle on the side."

She crinkled her nose and laughed out loud, then sobered and asked nonchalantly, "Is it because you were hungry for a long time, too?"

"Emma," Izzy said, scolding her daughter softly.

But it was too late. Michael stilled when he realized the girl showed signs of malnutrition: dark circles under her eyes, hollow depressions below her cheekbones, wrists the size of his pinky.

"That was a long time ago," Izzy said, placing a mug in front of him.

"How long?"

"Cream and sugar?" she asked, evading his question.

What could've brought her to Santa Fe? It was one of the most expensive places to live in the US, according to his personal observations, which bore no resemblance to scientific data in the least. He glanced at the duffel bag. They had food now, too. He wondered how her circumstances had changed so drastically. Did her ex starve them? Is that why she ran?

His hackles were rising, and he didn't even know what hackles were. "How about we make a deal?"

She put some nondairy creamer and a sugar bowl on the table, then sat across from him, her own cup in hand. "What kind of deal?"

"How about you answer my questions, and I don't call the cops for assault?" He would never call the police, but she didn't know that.

Her body stiffened with the threat, but she pretended to be unfazed and doctored her coffee with meticulous care before answering. "I'm sorry. I mistook you for someone else. Can you leave, and we'll just call it even?"

"Not today, Cupcake."

She looked up in surprise. Or desperation. He wasn't the very best at reading people.

"I'll find another place to stay," she pleaded. "We never have to see each other again."

No way in hell was that happening. "Answer my questions, and I'll think about it," he lied.

She pressed her lips together and went back to her coffee. "I don't know if I can address them all."

"What do you say we give it a shot?"

She lifted a shoulder as she stirred, the weight she carried darkening her features. "I get to ask questions, too?"

"Of course, but unlike you, I live a pretty boring life," said the guy living in a compound with the child of two gods, at least three ghosts, and a man who could see the last moments of a person's life on Earth. And that wasn't counting a deceased rottweiler named Artemis, twelve hellhounds, and countless other *talented* humans.

She took a long draw of her coffee, glancing at him from over the rim, then refocused on the cup as she set it in front of her. "You first."

"Again. Who's after you?"

"My ex."

So, he'd been right. "Why?"

"Because he's an asshole."

"Did he hurt Emma?"

Startled, Izzy's gaze darted back to his. "No," she said, shaking her head. "I would never have allowed that."

Thank God for small favors. "Why did you tell me she wasn't your daughter? Because of him?"

She dropped her gaze again and swallowed hard before answering. "Yes. He doesn't know about her. I left before she was born. He had no idea I was even pregnant."

"And you thought I would tell him about her?"

"Yes."

"Why? What makes you think I even know him?"

She bit her lip, and he saw the tension his question had caused when the muscles in her jaw hardened.

"Would he try to take her from you?"

"No." The smile that slid across her face held more sadness than a deflated balloon. "He would never do that."

"Then why don't you want him to find out about her?" He leaned closer. "Would he hurt her?"

The smile held steady as she shook her head. "Not in the way you think."

"Okay, then in what way?"

"It doesn't matter." She took another sip as Emma grabbed an apple and sat at the table with them.

He was growing frustrated. Getting information from Izzy was like pulling teeth with chopsticks, so he decided to circle back to his original line of questioning.

"Why did you think he'd found you when I showed up?"

She hesitated. Cleared her throat. Pulled at a thread on her shirt.

"Really?" he asked, his tone sharper than intended. "Nothing?"

She pushed away from the table and put her half-empty cup in the sink, her willowy frame seeming frail for the first time. Had she starved, as well? A burst of heat rushed through him at the thought.

He decided to push her. If she tased him again, he probably deserved it. But if she ran now, he may never have another chance. He may never get answers. She may never be safe. "I don't mean to sound like an asshole, Killer, but after what I've been through, I think I'm owed an explanation."

She scoffed and turned to look at him, bracing her hands on the sink's edge behind her. "Really? Someone like you, with your lifestyle? Are you sure you deserve anything?"

Another clue. He pondered her words for a long moment. "My *lifestyle*," he said, deep in thought.

"You guys stick together like saltwater taffy, right?"

"You guys?" he asked, feigning offense.

"Isn't that your thing?"

As they spoke, the squirt's head swiveled back and forth on her tiny body as though she were watching a tennis match. He barricaded his heart. If he wanted answers, now was not the time to cave to their charms.

"Who, exactly, are '*you guys*?'"

She gestured to his entire being with a sweep of her hand, like he disgusted her. It wouldn't be the first time, but this one kind of hurt.

He grabbed his heart—not literally—and raised his brows askance.

After a long moment, she huffed out a breath—the act far too sexy for his peace of mind—and pointed at...his arm?

He wore a white T-shirt and jeans with heavy boots. Had he ridden his bike over, he would also have a jacket on. But he hadn't, so he didn't. Thus, his arms were visible. Making his plethora of tattoos—some he was actually proud of—visible, as well. But he couldn't tell which one she had taken such offense to. The dogs playing cards—classic—or maybe the skull with a snake slithering through its eyes? He shook his head. "Look, I'm fairly sure I'm concussed, thanks to the frying pan thing. Can you be more specific?"

She scoffed once more, and he made a mental note to do as many annoying things to her as possible, so she did it again. She stepped forward and pointed at his motorcycle club's official tattoo. His *former* motorcycle club.

The squirt leaned over him to get a better view, apple crunching in her mouth. "Oh, I like that one," she said, running her fingers over the artwork. It was the official mark of a nationwide bike club called the Bandits. A triangle with a skull inside and two swords crossing under it, very similar to the international sign for poison. No one had ever accused the Bandits of being creative.

He had an appointment this week for a full cover-up. In two days, to be exact. None of this would've happened if he'd already gotten it done. She would never have seen the tattoo, tased him, or taken a frying pan to his skull. She wouldn't have leaned against him with those thighs.

What were the odds that he would get a call the very day he made the appointment? The artist, a good friend of his, had a cancellation and was able to get him in. Usually, it took months to get in with her, friend or not.

He thought back to the phone call he'd gotten at two this morning. The frantic voice. The frantic *young* voice.

Realization dawned, and a sense of astonishment sent an arctic chill up his spine. No way.

After grinding his teeth to dust, he scrubbed his fingers over his face, winced at the lump on the side of his head, and groaned. He was going to kill her. Elwyn Loehr. Had she really called him at two in the morning with a false report? How had he not recognized her voice? That little shit.

A harsh laugh escaped him. The girl was good. He'd give her that. And she'd been planning this for a while. No one else at the compound seemed to have picked up on her odd activities, but it was all becoming as clear as vodka to him. She would have waited until his maintenance tech was out, of course, but she had to make sure to get him to this apartment before his tattoo cover-up appointment.

But how? *How* did she know? About Izzy's ex. About the doctor Donovan had hooked up with. About the woman being stalked in Idaho, who Eric was now dating—happily. And now Michael and Izzy? Was this like a blind date?

First, if that was indeed her plan, the kid had good taste. But Michael had no supernatural abilities. Did that mean Izzy *did*? Did Elwyn need Izzy on her team? Did she want to add her to the list of soldiers for the upcoming war?

Every muscle in his body clenched at the thought of Izzy being in that kind of danger. He didn't want her anywhere near his mystical band of misfits.

Like he'd thought earlier, the kid was collecting supernaturally inclined humans, gathering her army, readying for a battle prophesied years ago. The mere thought of that child going to war with the king of the underworld gave him acid reflux. They needed more time. She needed more training. And he needed a lot more alcohol.

"So, he's a Bandit?" he asked.

She crossed her arms over her chest and turned to look out the window without answering.

"And you think we all know each other?"

"Don't you?" She turned back to him, the accusation clear in her tone *and* expression. Hostile. Defiant. Wildly beautiful. She swept her hair off her face with one gesture, the rich color of her eyes shimmering softly in the glow of the early morning sun. She'd been hurt. Badly.

Guard the heart, Cavalcante. Don't cave now.

"What's his name? We may be besties, and I just never made the connection."

A bitter smirk lifted one corner of her mouth, and he noticed tiny, almost imperceptible scars on the sides of it. "Dunsworth. Ross Dunsworth."

He shook his head. "Sorry, Killer. Doesn't ring a bell."

She didn't know if she should believe him or not. He could see it in the suspicious slant of her eyes. The thinning of her mouth.

Before he could question her further, the sound of heavy breathing filtered into his thoughts, and he looked at Emma. "You okay, Squirt?"

He glanced back at Izzy. A flash of fear registered on her face. She lunged forward and knelt beside her daughter. "Did you wash that apple, hon?"

"No. You already washed it. I saw you."

"Sweetheart, we've talked about this." Izzy pursed her lips and shook her head as though chastising herself. "I'm sorry. This is not your fault. Sit here, and I'll get your inhaler." She started to rise but whirled back around at the Squirt's next words.

"It's empty," she said as she coughed into a tiny hand.

"Empty?" Izzy squeaked, kneeling down to her again. "Since when?"

"Since I said, 'Mommy, my inhaler is empty.' We were supposed to pick up a new one today."

"Right." She pinched the bridge of her nose. "Okay, we'll go get it now." She checked the watch on her wrist. "They should be open, right? It's not too early?"

Emma rubbed her chest as the wheezing sound grew louder. "Mommy, I don't feel good."

Izzy pushed a plethora of curls off the girl's cheeks to expose how bright they'd become. Her jaw dropped as her gaze first locked onto Michael's and then darted to her purse. She dove for it, but Emma had closed her eyes and started sliding off the table.

Chapter Three

Please stop asking me if I've had a rough night.
I always look like this.
—Meme

"What's going on?" Michael asked Izzy as he scooped Emma into his arms and pulled her to his chest. She'd gone limp in a matter of seconds, and Izzy was doing everything in her power to quash the panic rising in her chest.

"She's having an allergic reaction," she said as she tore through her purse.

"To what?" he asked.

At last. Her fingers curled around the cylinder. She brought out an EpiPen and knelt in front of Michael, her baby completely limp and covered in hives. "Are you ready, sweetheart?"

Without opening her eyes, Emma nodded, the movement weak and hardly reassuring. But the Neanderthal was right. To what? She'd been eating an apple.

"Do you have peanuts in your pocket?" Izzy asked as she pushed the pen into Emma's thigh.

Though Emma didn't react to the needle, her airway relaxed almost instantly, just in time for her to throw up into her mouth. The fluid slipped past her swollen lips and ran down her cheek.

Izzy started to grab her, but Michael turned her over as she cleared her daughter's mouth and wiped her face. She was like a rag doll.

"I don't have peanuts. Where's your car?" he asked, standing with her cradled in his arms and heading toward the door.

Izzy grabbed her keys and purse and followed. "Any kind of energy bar with peanuts in it?"

"No." He didn't wait for the elevator. He headed straight for the stairs and rushed down them with surprising agility, given his size.

"Have you been eating peanuts?"

He stopped just outside the building and looked for her parking space. "Is that yours? The Hyundai?"

"Yes, but if you've been eating peanuts, you're only hurting her more."

"Let me guess," he said as she unlocked the doors. "She's allergic to peanuts." He opened the back door and grabbed Izzy's arm, shoving her into the back seat.

"Yes, and—"

"No. I haven't had any." He looked into Emma's face. "Her eyes are swelling up."

Michael handed Emma to her, then pulled out the seat belt and fastened it around both of them. He took the keys out of Izzy's hand and closed the door.

"We should call an ambulance," she said when he jumped into the driver's seat, hurriedly pushing it back so he wasn't eating the steering wheel, and then started the car.

"Trust me, Killer. I'm much faster." And he was. He cornered and switched lanes like they were on glass.

Izzy held Emma to her, checking her breathing and making sure her airway was clear, or as clear as possible, but the wheezing had her stomach twisting into Gordian knots.

"Does this happen often?" he asked.

"No. Not like this. I don't understand. It was just an apple."

"But she reacted right after taking a couple of bites."

"I wash every piece of produce before putting it out, just in case. I can't imagine how this happened."

He had them in front of the emergency room in four minutes. It would've taken an ambulance longer than that just to get to them. He jumped out of the car, took Emma into his arms, and ran inside, leaving Izzy to follow once again, her heart swelling almost painfully with gratitude.

"Severe allergic reaction," he called out to a nurse, placing Emma onto a gurney. "And she has asthma."

The nurse checked Emma's pupils and called for a colleague as she wheeled the gurney back to the emergency room. "How long has she been unconscious?"

"About five minutes," Izzy said, following closely. "Her inhaler is empty. I gave her a shot with an EpiPen. It helped, but then she started vomiting and passed out." The longer she spoke, the more her voice rose. Panic darkened the edges of her vision.

"What's her name?"

"Emma. Emma Walsh."

"Emma? Can open your eyes for me, sweetheart?" the nurse said loudly, getting no response. She checked Emma's vitals and made sure her airway was clear as two other nurses and a doctor rushed over. The wheezing was better but still there.

"What's she allergic to?" the doctor asked, checking her pupils yet again.

"Peanuts."

"Did she eat any?"

"Of course, not," she said. "I don't keep them in the house."

"Peanut butter left on a spoon?"

"Never. I don't keep peanut products in the house at all." What did he care at this point anyway? He needed to focus on her daughter and stop accusing her of being a bad mother. She could do that all by herself.

The doctor, looking younger than the gray at his temples suggested, ran his stethoscope over Emma's chest and checked the meter clipped to her finger. "Let's get her some oxygen, start an IV with Benadryl, and I need that epinephrine. Now."

"Yes, Doctor," an older nurse said, her every move like a well-oiled machine.

They took scissors to Emma's shirt, the incision cutting the head off a sparkly unicorn, her tiny body startlingly fragile on the huge gurney. As an army of medical professionals worked on Emma, Michael put his hands on Izzy's shoulders and pulled her back a little to give them room. The warmth of his palms startled her. As did the reassurance his closeness brought. She'd felt like a sparrow in a hurricane for so long, navigating a never-ending barrage of distrust and threats. She didn't know how to take this new sensation.

At some point, a woman from administration came to get Emma's insurance card along with Izzy's ID, but they didn't ask Izzy to leave her daughter's side to fill out the paperwork just yet. For that, she was thankful.

It didn't take long for Emma to wake up. They talked to her, speaking clearly to make sure she was responsive. Her eyes looked huge over the mask administering a breathing treatment, but she nodded her head and answered everything she could—in her British accent, of course—until she could no longer fight the weight of her lids and they drifted shut again.

The hives had disappeared, and the swelling in her face had diminished. They draped her in a pink hospital gown with rabbits on it, and a nurse covered her in a warm blanket as the doctor, almost as tall as the man at her back, pulled them aside.

"We're going to keep her overnight for observation. Her symptoms could return, but she seems to be out of the woods."

Izzy breathed deeply for the first time since they'd arrived. It had felt as though Emma's condition had manifested in Izzy's body, fighting for the air she couldn't allow it to have.

"You don't know how this happened?" he asked.

She shook her head. "I'm very careful, and she hasn't been out of the house since yesterday. I can't imagine."

"Okay, well, Stacy is bringing you the papers to get her registered. But just so you know, we have to report this."

"Report it?" Michael said, closing the distance between them to stand beside her as though readying to confront the doctor.

She patted his hand, the one on her right shoulder, to calm him. Of course, they had to report the incident. It was protocol. Izzy knew about the allergy, and Emma had been in her care when it happened. Child abuse? Neglect? They had no way of knowing that she would die for the tiny creature lying in that bed.

She pressed her lips together and nodded. "I know."

The doctor smiled sadly. "I take it this isn't your first rodeo."

"It's not," she said, lifting her chin. Short and sweet. For now, her goal was to keep their conversation as concise as possible. The paperwork would be a nightmare. She just wanted to get through it and focus on Emma, not answer his questions on top of the plethora that awaited her.

The doctor nodded to her, then to Michael, the Neanderthal, whose hands were still on her shoulders like they belonged there, the warmth the most comforting thing she'd felt in a very long time. She'd had no one. Absolutely no one. And then he'd shown up like he owned the place—which he did—and went from hostage to confidante in a matter of hours. How was this happening?

"We'll take her to her room now," a nurse said. Izzy hadn't noticed when the doctor left. "You can bring this paperwork with you." She handed Michael at least a tree's worth of papers secured to a bright-orange clipboard.

He accepted them.

"We'll come get it in a bit. Take your time."

"Is she completely out of the woods?" Michael asked her.

"Her symptoms can return even stronger hours after an initial reaction. It's called biphasic anaphylaxis."

"I'll take your word for that."

"If you notice any changes in her breathing, hives, swelling, if she complains of dizziness, anything like that, call the nurse immediately." She and a colleague pushed the gurney down a bright hallway to an oversized elevator. She selected the third floor and added, "But we'll be close by if you'd like to get coffee or grab some breakfast."

"Maybe later," he said, never taking his eyes off Emma. Izzy realized he had an arm around her shoulders, steering her down the hall.

The feeling of having someone with her, of not being utterly alone, was new. It was both unsettling and oddly comforting. She chastised herself—she had no idea who this man was—and tried to put some space between them. He let her, yet kept a hand lightly on her upper back as though knowing she needed the support. Was she so transparent?

They took Emma to a room in the pediatrics wing. It had a recliner that doubled as a bed so a parent could stay the night. The nurses flitted around Emma, getting her settled before heading out.

One of them turned back, a pretty blonde who couldn't seem to take her eyes off of Michael. "There's also coffee and soda right down the hall." She pointed. "There's usually pastries, too. And there's always ice cream in the freezer if you need a pick-me-up."

"Thank you," Izzy said, wondering if the man she'd assaulted not more than five hours earlier had noticed the girl's interest. Not that it mattered to her.

Michael pulled one of the two chairs closer to Emma's bed and motioned for her to sit, then went around and grabbed the second one for himself. They sat on either side of Emma, facing each other, and Izzy did everything in her power to avoid eye contact. She smoothed the blanket. Checked the IV on the back of Emma's hand. Reached over to adjust the canula under her nose and over her ears so it didn't pull and cause soreness. Then she remembered the paperwork and stretched to grab the clipboard on the windowsill behind her when he spoke, his voice harder than she'd expected.

"She felt like feathers."

She turned back to him, his stare accusatory.

"She weighs nothing. Why is she so thin?"

Izzy couldn't help the emotions his questions stirred inside her. He knew nothing about them, yet his words sank into her chest like a knife. It tightened, and her bottom lip trembled. She pulled it between her teeth to stop it. He had no idea what they'd been through. How dare he accuse her of…what? Abuse? Neglect?

Then she looked at Emma. The tiny being that made her life worth living. Emma had never let their circumstances crush her spirit. She was Izzy's light. Her sun. Her reason for living. Now, she understood how a mother could give up her life to save her child. She would do that very thing a thousand times if that's what it took to keep her daughter safe.

"Izzy," Michael prompted.

She shook out of her thoughts but didn't dare look at him. She didn't think she could take any more accusations, and this was not the time or place to launch into defense mode. So, she simply said, "She's five."

He didn't buy it. "I know what a five-year-old girl weighs."

Surprised, she looked up at him and made a disgusted face to try to throw him off course. "That doesn't sound creepy at all."

His expression flatlined. "My charge was five years old."

Wonderful. A change in direction. She'd take it. "Your charge?"

"The daughter of two of my best friends. I'm part of her security team."

"Security? That's your job?"

"One of them. As I was saying—"

"Wait, she *was* five years old? How old is she now?"

He narrowed his eyes on her, probably figuring out her game. "Fourteen. Ish. But she was five not that long ago."

Izzy frowned. "She was five nine years ago."

He drew in a deep breath and went back to watching Emma like a wolf watches its prey, not waiting for the symptoms to return but hunting them down before they dared show themselves. "It's a long story," he said, his voice soft, his expression contemplative. "Suffice it to say I know what a five-year-old with more attitude than a runway model in Gucci weighs." She smiled at his startlingly accurate description of her daughter, until he added, "So, what's her story?"

How could she explain the complexities of their lives without giving away the truth? "We haven't always had an easy life."

After a long moment, he looked back at her, his gaze somber, and she realized how incredibly handsome he was. Eyes like sunshine on the Mediterranean Sea, so blue they were startling. A nose almost imperceptibly crooked, much like the smile he'd cast her more than once that day. And a strong, shadowed jaw that begged to be touched like the sharp side of a machete begging to be tested. All brooding charisma and rugged charm. He could handle himself in a fight. That much was clear. He had a boxer's shoulders and a perceptive nature—almost wary, from what she'd seen so far.

But those types of people tended to lean toward violence to solve their problems. Just like her ex. Then again, he didn't have the calmness this guy had. Like a hand grenade, powerful and explosive, sitting quietly, biding its time until all else failed and power was needed. He may have been a member of the infamous Bandits, but he was probably one of the more levelheaded of the bunch. Did that make him less dangerous? Or more?

"Why?" he asked, his tone gentle but stern.

"Why?"

"Why hasn't your life been easy?"

"In a word?"

He lifted one of those boxer's shoulders. "Sure."

"Men."

That crooked smile emerged, one corner of his shapely mouth rising, and she steeled her heart. She and Emma did not need a man in their lives. Never again.

"Care to elaborate?"

"I hate to be the bearer of bad news, *Cupcake*," she said, referencing his earlier use of the colloquialism, "but I don't owe you anything."

He reached up and rubbed his temple. The one that had darkened from the trauma it'd received.

What had she been thinking? She hadn't. Plain and simple. She'd gotten a knock at two in the morning. Nobody thought well at two in the morning. Both her brain and body had reverted to their most basic survival mechanism: sheer panic. Maybe because of all the strange things that had been happening to her over the past couple of weeks. She'd been on edge, a razor-sharp one, and it wasn't helping her stress levels.

She dropped her gaze and took Emma's hand. "Sorry about that."

"Don't be. I deserve a lot worse than a frying pan to the skull."

"Yeah?" Her gaze met his again. "What have you done?"

"What *haven't* I done?" he said with a comical snort. "But, back to the topic at hand…"

She swallowed hard. "I'm sorry. There are some things I can't talk about."

"I could always file assault charges."

By now, she knew that particular threat was just that. A threat and nothing more. His reaction when the doctor said he had to report the incident told her everything she needed to know. He didn't like the authorities, in any way, shape, or form. She would use that to her advantage.

"And I could always report your building for code violations."

He'd been leaning forward against the bed, his elbows resting beside Emma, but he shot straight up at her words, a look of utter dismay on his face. She had to fight tooth and nail not to giggle. He really was too easy.

"What code violations? I've been really careful. Some would even say meticulous."

She lifted a single brow and gave him a judgmental once-over. "Not careful enough, I guess."

"Mommy," Emma said, her voice hoarse.

"Emma!" Izzy threw an arm over her daughter and leaned closer.

Emma's lips were chapped, her face had grown ashen, and when she finally pried them open, her eyes were watery and lined in red.

A sharp pang of regret rocketed through her. She pushed the curls back from Emma's face. "Sweetheart, are you okay?"

She placed a hand on one of Izzy's that cupped her face. Izzy grabbed hold of it and brought it to her mouth, kissing each tiny knuckle over and over.

"I told you. He's made of light. We can trust him. Even Celie says so, and she doesn't even like him."

"Celie?" Michael asked. He stood and looked down at the two of them, relief softening his strong features.

Izzy ignored him and turned back to her daughter. "Then how did he—?" She stopped and glanced at him once more before lowering her voice and leaning closer. "How did he…you know, do what he did?"

Emma frowned and eyed him through squinted lids. "I don't know, Mommy. You should tie him up and torture him for information."

"I'm game," he said.

Izzy rolled her eyes, but the little miscreant in the bed just giggled. Then coughed. Her chest sounded like gravel, and she struggled to take a deep breath.

They both pulled her into a sitting position, and Michael rubbed her back while Izzy poured her a cup of water. After a quick sip, Emma calmed down and lay back in the bed.

"Is this normal?" he asked Izzy. "Should we call the nurse?"

Emma shook her head and said between coughs, "It's okay. They're very busy."

"Hey." He took her chin between his thumb and index finger and turned her face toward him. "Not too busy for you, kiddo. Never too busy for you."

His words surprised Izzy yet again. How could he be so caring toward a girl he'd only known a couple of hours? Her brain could not reconcile the man who'd once been a biker in a notoriously violent motorcycle club with the gentle giant sitting across from her now. It just didn't compute.

The young nurse came into the room, pushing a wheelchair. "Looks like I'm just in time," she said, her gaze darting from Emma to Michael.

He didn't seem to notice.

Izzy rose to her feet. "Where are you taking her?"

"The doctor would like an X-ray of her chest for precautionary measures," she said. To Michael, completely ignoring the woman who'd been in labor for twenty-four hours just to bring the patient into the world.

Izzy convinced her eyes not to roll back too far lest she look possessed. "Okay." She nodded her approval and lifted Emma out of the bed. "She's been coughing."

"We'll get another breathing treatment ready."

"Thank you." Michael helped her put Emma in the wheelchair before folding a blanket and draping it over her bare legs.

"You good, Squirt?"

She nodded and gave him a thumbs-up before coughing into her hand again.

"I should go with her, don't you think?" Izzy said.

"This'll just take a minute. I'll have her back in a jiff."

The nurse smiled sweetly at Michael and started to leave, but Izzy didn't like the girl's answer, even though she had no reason to argue. The last thing she wanted to do was draw attention to their already precarious situation, but her anxiety took hold, so she made a decision. One that might look strange to the unindoctrinated, but better safe than sorry.

She hurried to hold the door as the nurse pushed the chair over the threshold, but before they got far, Izzy put a hand on the girl's shoulder.

The nurse turned to her, confused.

Just the opening she needed. She locked gazes with her, lowered her voice, and said, "Be still."

The nurse stilled instantly, her face going slack.

"You will not take your eyes off my daughter, even for a second, until you have brought her back to me safe and sound. Do you understand?"

"Yes," the girl said, her eyes watering due to her inability to blink. "Completely."

"That will be all," Izzy said.

The nurse blinked back to reality, nodded hesitantly, then pushed the wheelchair toward the elevators, offering one last glance over her shoulder before pressing the button.

"That was interesting."

Izzy jumped two feet into the air. The Neanderthal had walked up behind her and had seen the whole exchange.

"What?" she asked as nonchalantly as she could manage.

"You do that a lot. Give people strange orders and expect them to follow them."

She scoffed and walked back into the room to get her purse. She sat to send a text, letting her boss know she wouldn't be in, and then scrolled through the phone to call Emma's school to report her absence. Emma had only just started there three weeks ago. She hated that she had to miss already, but it was Friday, and they were letting the kids out early for in-service, so she shouldn't miss much.

But she'd only started her job at the diner three weeks ago. She could be fired for this. Her stomach churned at the thought. She could always order her boss to reinstate her, but she hated doing that. It was unfair, and who knew what it did to their brains? She tried to only use her ability in emergency situations. Like with the nurse. Desperate times and all.

Also, she liked the owner. He and his wife had practically saved her life. She would never be able to repay them.

"It would seem we have a little time on our hands," the Neanderthal said, taking his seat on the other side of the bed. "Maybe we could pick up where we left off."

"You and I both know you won't call the cops."

"No, but I could always call my old buddy Ross Dunsworth."

Izzy sucked in a soft breath. The threat did exactly what the man wanted it to, and it told her all she needed to know about him. "I knew I should never have trusted you."

He shrugged. "Live and learn. Now, spill."

A sting behind her eyes had her fighting tears of frustration. The threat may have seemed unremarkable to the Neanderthal, but she had been running for her life—for Emma's life—for six years. There was nothing unremarkable about Ross Dunsworth. The man was ruthless. He would stop at nothing to get what he wanted, and he wanted nothing more than Izzy's head on a platter. Along with the rest of her. Because how else would she be useful to him?

And Emma. Oh, how he would use her to his advantage, just like he had with Izzy's sister. She would die before she put Emma into such a precarious situation, and Izzy knew exactly what to do with her precious daughter should it come to that. She already had people picked out to raise her. They were an older couple, so gentle and kind, and they loved Emma like their own daughter.

But she would avoid that situation if she could, and that meant dealing with Michael. She didn't want to run again. She had a sweet setup in Santa Fe, but she could waitress at any diner in the country. Jobs weren't the problem. Making enough money for food and shelter was.

She welded her teeth together in resignation and swallowed hard before starting. This man could be the death of her. One phone call, and the fragile world she'd built would come tumbling down around her. Her hands shook ever-so-slightly, and she laced her fingers together to stop it before raising her chin as defiantly as she could. "Just so you know, I will never be controlled again."

He lifted a single brow. "I would hope not."

"I'm very smart."

"I've noticed."

"And I'm not afraid to hurt anyone who tries to take advantage of me or my daughter."

"Good."

She let a bitter smile steal across her face. "You'll change your mind once you know the truth. Greed gets the better of even the strongest men."

He leaned closer, staring at her from over the bed as he softly said, "You don't know me very well, Killer, so I'll let that slide."

Surprised by his offense, she tried to figure him out. No one in her entire life, not one person, had ever been immune to her ability. But this man with his cerulean eyes and ridiculously wide shoulders was. She had never seen anything like it. And now he was about to find out the truth. A man she had no control over would know her secret.

Every bone in her body screamed for her to run. To get Emma, leave all their possessions behind, and just go. But her daughter had said she could trust him, and Emma had never been wrong. She'd even saved their lives once with that nifty trick of hers. She had the ability to assess someone's mettle in a matter of seconds. She could see anger, grief, jealousy, and happiness from a mile away. She was extraordinary, and Izzy would never let anyone use her like she had been used. Their gifts couldn't be more different, yet they could both be used to do horrible things. But Emma trusted this man. Seemed to adore him. And that was very rare.

Still, her bones were screaming, the muscles around them straining for her to get up. To run. To hunt down Emma and disappear like she'd done so many times before.

Maybe it was worth one more shot. What could it hurt, after all? She had to try. For Emma, she needed to try.

She leaned close to him, as well, and concentrated as hard as she could on the man before her. "You will forget me and my daughter in fifteen seconds."

"This again?" he asked, seemingly disappointed.

"You will get up immediately and walk out of this hospital."

"I don't think so, Cupcake." He blinked. He didn't get up and walk out, he blinked.

Damn it. She couldn't give up now. "You will forget everything that has happened today."

"I don't know if you know this, but being tased is rather unforgettable."

"And you will…" She huffed out a breath of defeat. "Why are you not leaving?"

"No way can I leave now. This is just getting good."

"Who are you?" she asked as though he could tell her why he was immune to her ability.

He reached a hand over the bed for her to shake. "Cavalcante. Michael Cavalcante. Though growing up, my friends called me GD."

She ignored his hand. "GD?" she asked, remembering the tattoo on the inside of his forearm with the letters GD inside a pair of salivating canine teeth, the dog behind them a Rottweiler. A mercurial moment of déjà vu flitted across her mind, like trying to grab a handful of fog and having it slip through her fingers.

He shrugged and folded his arms over his chest. "Long story. How about we get back to our regularly scheduled program?"

She gave up. She had no choice. It wasn't like telling him the truth would change anything. He wouldn't believe her. They never did. At first. It was only after they began to believe her that the trouble started, and she had no intention of proving herself. Basically, she was making a mountain out of a molehill. A deadly, cancerous molehill.

She drew in a deep breath and said, "I've done terrible things."

"Who hasn't? Keep going."

"No, really. I've hurt people."

"Sounds like you didn't have much of a choice if someone was controlling you."

She dropped her gaze to study her scuffed boots. "That doesn't excuse everything."

"How about you explain, and I'll give you my two cents? If you want them. But don't spend them all in one place," he added, warning her with an index finger.

He was impossible. All charm and charisma. She didn't owe him anything, but she decided to give him a heads-up nonetheless. "You won't like it."

"I never liked eating vegetables either, but what can you do?"

Or maybe he would. Fine. He wanted the truth? He would get the truth. She tossed him a challenging glare and said point-blank, "I began robbing banks when I was seven."

Chapter Four

I've never had a problem I couldn't make worse.
—True story

"*Seven*?" Michael asked. Of all the things he'd imagined she would say, robbing banks while still in elementary school had not made the list.

"Seven," she confirmed. She picked up the paperwork and began filling it out.

"Seven sheets to the wind because you're a lush?" he guessed, unable to process her statement. Trying to rob a bank drunk seemed plausible. He'd certainly done worse in an inebriated state.

"Seven years old," she clarified. "Before that, it was convenience stores." She checked a box. "Pawn shops." Check. "Liquor stores." Check, check, check. "But my stepfather wanted bigger scores, so banks it was."

Michael stared at her for a long moment, trying to decide whether to believe her or not. He'd determined early on that she was a little off her rocker. Maybe she was more off the thing than he'd imagined. Perhaps she'd taken a sledgehammer to it and used it for firewood.

"Iz," he said, trying to be as gentle as possible, "can I call you Iz? You're hardly intimidating now. How did you manage to rob banks at seven?" And why had it never made the evening news? A story like that would have been on *60 Minutes*, for sure. Or, at the very least, the *National Enquirer.*

She stared back at him, and he figured it was fair. He'd done it first, those eyes so mesmerizing he had a hard time *not* staring. "Like I said, I was forced."

He laughed under his breath and scooted farther down in his chair.

"Okay, I'll bite. We have way more in common than I thought. Another long story. Only I certainly didn't start at seven."

"You robbed banks?"

"Let's just say, someone was controlling me. And my friends. But enough about me…"

"No, this is really interesting," she said, trying to distract him. She lowered the pen and leaned forward to encourage him.

He was easy, but he wasn't *that* easy. "How old were you the first time you *assisted* your stepfather?"

She picked up the pen again, her lower lip jutting in disappointment. "Five."

Every muscle in his body tensed despite her charming pout, but he did everything in his power not to show his knee-jerk reaction. "And this has something to do with an ability?"

She pressed her lips together. It hardly detracted from their fullness. "Yes."

"So, you give people orders, and they just follow them?"

"Yes. Everyone." She glanced up at him. "Everyone but you."

"Why?"

She scoffed. "You tell me. No one has ever been able to disobey my orders. Ever."

That was strange, but he'd been referring to the ability. "I mean, why would anyone follow your orders?"

"I don't know. They just always have. Since I was little."

"What did your parents do?"

"Anything I wanted them to."

He nodded in understanding, seeing before she explained the fragile circumstances that could create.

"Do you know what a two-year-old with that kind of power is capable of? One who has no sense of right and wrong? No sense of morality?" She shook her head and went back to the paperwork. "My poor mom."

"How did she deal with it?"

A small smile crept across her pretty face as she worked. "Headphones."

He laughed.

She joined him. "We literally learned sign language and used it for most things until I was old enough to know right from wrong. But even then… I put that poor woman through hell." Her smile faded as she thought back. "That's how my mom met my stepdad. He had a Deaf aunt. She was teaching sign language classes in a town near us, and my mom took one—

with me in tow, of course. Her nephew showed up one night to help her with the projector and spotted my mom. She was such a beauty."

"I can imagine."

She shook out of her thoughts. "They hit it off, and the rest is history."

"So, it's auditory? The sign language didn't work?"

"I couldn't mesmerize at first because I didn't know how to use it to get what I wanted. Later, even the sign language became an issue for my mom. I was incorrigible."

He blinked in surprise. "You can give orders using sign language, too?"

"Yes, but I'm not very good. I once told a Deaf boy to stop being rude. At least, I thought I did. He stripped naked in front of me. Apparently, hand placement is very important in ASL."

He rubbed his mouth to hide his grin. "And your biological father?"

"He was never in the picture. My mom never told me what happened, but she ended up marrying my stepfather when I was around four."

"And he saw a way to make a quick buck," Michael said, seeing all too clearly how that would've scarred her from a very young age.

She nodded. "When my mother found out, she tried to take me and leave." Her brows slid together, ostensibly in response to a difficult question on the papers in her lap, but she wasn't fooling him. He spotted the telltale wetness between her lashes. She cleared her throat and added, "He killed her for it. For me. To keep control of the goose that laid the golden eggs."

Michael didn't move, didn't speak, lest he give away the dark emotions churning inside him. He gave her a moment before questioning her further. He could definitely see why Elwyn had chosen Izzy. She would be a powerful ally in the coming tribulations, but the last thing Michael wanted was for this lovely woman to get mixed up in their lives. Their very dangerous, incredibly volatile lives.

"Did he tell you he killed her?" he asked, hopeful the man had lied and just abducted Izzy, leaving her mother alive and searching for her daughter for over two decades. It was better than the alternative.

She gripped the pen so hard her knuckles turned white. "He didn't have to. I saw the whole thing."

Damn it. "I'm sorry, Iz."

She glanced up in surprise. "It's okay. It was a long time ago."

"Yeah, that's not something you just get over."

"True, but I have Emma now. I can get over anything if it means keeping her safe."

His admiration of her knew no bounds. She was a badass. "What happened to him? Your stepfather?"

"I eventually escaped and went to the police. I told them everything. Well, not how we robbed banks and such, but everything about the murder. They investigated and arrested him three days later. He's been rotting in prison in North Carolina ever since."

"How old were you?"

"Ten. From there, I was in and out of so many foster homes, I became a walking cliché."

He shook his head. "There is no way you could ever be a walking cliché. Still, that was very brave."

"Not really. He had no leverage over me apart from his paltry threats. My ex was much smarter when it came to such things."

"In what way?"

She smiled sadly. "He had leverage. And he used it well. But he wasn't like that at first." Her gaze slid past him as the memories resurfaced. "He was so kind and attentive, and I…I had no one at the time. I was living on the streets when he saw me one night, and…it's complicated."

He didn't want to push her. How her ex had groomed her to be his doormat was not important for the time being. "So, there's an entire chapter of the Bandits that knows about your ability?" How many men would he have to take down?

"No. He never told them. He wanted me and my ability all to himself, so he kept them in the dark. He just told them I could talk my way into or out of any situation." She shrugged. "He wasn't lying."

"Why didn't you use your powers on them? Your stepfather and your ex."

"I did, but it often backfired."

"In what way?"

"My stepfather put the fear of God in me when he figured out that I'd once given him a directive. And Ross had safeguards in place."

"What kind of safeguards?"

"He figured out pretty quickly how it all worked. When I give a directive, it displaces time. Throws you off balance. The target senses it when they snap out of it and things aren't quite how they left them. So, Ross slowly figured out other ways to control me." She looked up and impaled him with an accusing glare. "Like you will probably try to do the minute you come up with a plan."

"You clearly don't know me very well."

"Don't tell me, you're not that kind of guy?"

"No, I'm just really bad at making plans, so you're safe with me. I try not to think that far ahead. What was the leverage?"

"The leverage?"

"You said earlier he had leverage. That's how he controlled you. What was it?"

"Oh, my sister." Her eyes instantly shimmered with emotion. "If I didn't do what he wanted, he threatened to put her in the hospital. He wouldn't kill her. That would defeat the purpose. But he would make sure she spent several days in intensive care." A bitter laugh escaped her at the thought. "Not that he would do it himself. He wasn't only a thief. He was a coward of the lowest form. He would have his cronies do it so he couldn't be implicated."

"What did he have you do?"

She huffed out a breath and shook her head, the memories clearly unpleasant. "At first, it was little things. Get him out of a speeding ticket. Convince a cashier to give him a carton of cigarettes. Tell one of his cronies to take money out of the MC president's safe for him."

"I take it the demands got worse over time?"

"Much. He was worse than my stepfather in some ways. And he had big plans. He wanted me to con older adults out of their life savings.

"Classy."

"I thought so. He was researching who to target, and all the while, I was having a complete mental breakdown."

Michael fought the urge to hunt the man down right then and there. First things first.

"I started planning, too," she continued. "How to keep my sister safe while getting him thrown in prison. I planned to set him up. I had a detective waiting in the wings. Then something horrible happened. The clubhouse was raided, and the higher-ups began suspecting Ross."

"Did he do it?"

"Not personally, but he was behind it. He fed a rival club member information about the layout of the clubhouse and how to get into the safe and weapons cache. He wanted to overthrow the Bandits' president, but some of the club members caught on to the fact that he was an absolute snake. He began worrying that his patsy would get caught and snitch on him, so he tried to get me to order the man to jump off a roof. That's when I knew I had to get away."

"Did you?"

"Get away?"

"Order the man to jump to his death."

She gasped softly and gaped at him. "I would never. I refused to be an accomplice to murder. I don't even know if it's possible. Self-preservation is a powerful thing."

Good for her, but… "How did Ross take that?"

She lowered her head and absently rubbed her arm. It didn't take a genius to know he'd hurt her. "Not well, but he gave in. I knew he was just biding his time. He had big dreams, and becoming the president of the North Carolina chapter was one of them. But he told me a couple of people had to die before that could happen."

"Sounds like you got out just in time," Michael said, straining to keep his tone neutral.

"By the skin of my teeth."

As he listened to Izzy's story, his breaths grew shallow as memories of his mother surfaced. They'd run, as well. The two of them. Not fast enough, however. Not far enough. "How did you escape him?" he asked, forcing the memories back into the filthy corners of his soul where they belonged.

"My foster sister, the only person on Earth who never used my ability to her advantage—not even when she failed a very important exam in high school—died suddenly."

"I'm sorry, Izzy." He picked up his chair and brought it around to the edge of the bed to be closer to her, wondering where this was going.

She didn't seem to notice. "She was my everything," she continued, lost in her memories. "He knew how much she meant to me and used that information for all it was worth."

"How did she die?"

She shook out of her thoughts and offered him a smile, desperately heavy with the burden of guilt. "It was all very convenient. The timing. The conditions. I told her I was pregnant and said I was going to leave Ross as soon as I could coordinate with the detective." She looked at Michael as though pleading for him to understand. "I never told her she was being used as leverage, but somehow, she figured it out. She must have. She was so smart that way."

"As are you."

She scoffed, the sound bitter in the sterile room. "Not like her. Two days after I told her about the pregnancy, she sent me a cryptic message. All emojis. A suitcase, a woman in sunglasses, a woman running, praying hands, and then about a thousand hearts followed by a poop emoji because she always sent me a poop emoji, no matter how serious the message. The next day, she died in a car accident, and I ran." A tear managed to slide past her lashes, leaving a silvery trail down her cheek. She wiped it off. "I didn't even go to her funeral. I knew he would be waiting for me, so I didn't get to see my sister, my best friend, off to the netherworld."

Michael found himself suffocating under the weight of Izzy's grief. He couldn't imagine how she felt. "Are you saying she killed herself to save you?"

"Possibly." She swiped at a curl that had fallen over her eyes and tucked it behind an ear, the movement sharp with annoyance. "Probably. She had stage four pancreatic cancer. Never smoked a day in her life. Ate healthy. Ran every chance she got. It made no sense. But Ross found out about her diagnosis. He was worried he would lose his leverage, and I knew I had to tell her soon. I had no idea she'd figured it out."

Michael couldn't imagine what it was like to grow up with such an ability. From the way she spoke, her stepfather and ex weren't the only people who'd used her for it. To be constantly betrayed by those she believed genuinely cared for her… No wonder she had trust issues.

"Can I ask how you robbed banks as a seven-year-old? How did you rob anything?"

"First, it was convenience stores. I would simply tell the cashier to forget us in sixty seconds, then tell them to give us all the money they had—no dye packs, of course. I will never make that mistake again. And then I told them to erase any video footage of our visit."

"Thorough."

"Always," she said, almost proud. "Banks weren't as easy. The tellers don't usually have access to the surveillance equipment. But even when the authorities watched the videos, I imagine they were confused. The tellers wouldn't have remembered anything about the robbery. I like to think they slept okay at night with no memory of such a traumatic event. Then again, maybe it was worse for them to not remember. To the authorities, we looked like a father and daughter just taking money out of the bank.

"Of course, that couldn't last forever. They eventually caught on, and we ended up on the FBI's most wanted list. Well, my stepdad did. They thought he was just using me as a prop to put the tellers at ease."

"How do you know all this?"

"I asked an FBI agent on the case."

"You just asked nicely, and they complied?"

She crinkled one corner of her mouth as though chastising him, a tiny dimple appearing out of nowhere to shred his heart. "I ordered her to tell me and then forget me. At my stepfather's behest, mind you. He tracked her down to a diner in Charlotte. I just walked up to her table and did my thing."

He sat back, shaking his head. He'd seen all manner of abilities, but this was a first. Still, Michael had a serious problem with Emma's allergic reaction. Something wasn't right, and they needed to get to the bottom of it. "I would love to know more, but we need to focus on one thing at a time."

"One thing?"

"You said strange things have been happening lately. How strange?"

"Just odd things that don't mean much alone. But they keep happening."

"Like?"

"Someone keyed my car the other day. I have no idea who. And two weeks ago, I was almost run down in a grocery store parking lot by an old rust bucket of a Jeep. The SUV kind. Not the sporty one."

He took out his phone to take notes. "What color?"

"Rust, mostly." When he raised his brows in question, she added, "Gray and very beat-up. It was at Smith's. The one on Cerrillos."

"Got it. What else?"

"Well, I keep losing tire pressure, but when I take it in, they swear I don't have a leak. Just strange events that don't mean much."

"But taken as a whole…"

"Exactly."

They had security cameras at the complex. He would check those first. "Do you think this Ross asshat has found you?"

She breathed out a sigh filled with frustration and concern. "I don't know. Ross isn't much of a thinker, you know? If he'd found me, I truly believe he would've come for me. He wouldn't play games. He wouldn't risk losing me again."

Michael nodded. "I agree."

"Wait." She set the completed paperwork aside and narrowed her gaze on him.

He didn't mind in the least.

"You're taking all of this really well."

"All of what?"

"Me. My ability. Even Emma's gift. You act like it's an everyday thing. You…you believe me."

"I've seen stranger things than you, Killer. And much scarier."

She smirked. "I don't know. I can be pretty scary."

"Not without a Taser in your hand. What was her name?"

"Whose name?"

"Your sister's?"

She smiled despite the gravity of the situation. It was a glorious thing, her smile. Wide and genuine, with full lips and a row of perfect teeth. That, combined with the color of her eyes, once again brought back a sense of familiarity. A longing. Did he know her from somewhere? Had he seen her in a grocery store or at a restaurant before all of this happened?

No. There was no way. He never would have forgotten those eyes.

She gazed at him, her face aglow with the memory of her sister, and said softly, "Emmaline," pronouncing the name carefully, precisely, as though it were a precious thing.

When it dawned on him that she'd named her daughter after her sister, his heart softened even more, the hard, sharp edges threatening to melt away. But he couldn't allow himself to get attached. His attraction was simply that, a physical draw to a beautiful woman. He didn't want her anywhere near the compound, or the little hellion clearly trying to recruit her.

Michael noticed the phones ringing first. He turned his head toward the nurse's desk across the hall. That alerted Izzy, and she straightened in her chair. When a strobe light began flashing in the hallway, their gazes locked for half a second before they both jumped to their feet and rushed into the hall.

Chapter Five

There are so many cool things I would do
if it weren't for the laws of physics.
And regular laws.
—Meme

"Where is my daughter?" Izzy asked as a nurse scrambled to answer phone call after phone call.

The nurse's startled expression at Izzy's question filled her with a deep sense of dread. Something had gone terribly wrong.

"Where is radiology?" Michael asked, almost yelling at her.

The older woman put a hand over the receiver and pointed toward the elevators. "First floor. Across from the labs."

Once again, he didn't wait for said elevator. Or Izzy, for that matter. He tore through the door to the stairwell and disappeared.

Izzy ran after him, but she couldn't think. Did Emma have another attack? Or was she still waiting for the X-ray machine to open up, and none of this had anything to do with her? Panic squeezed her chest tight and blurred her vision as Michael took the stairs one platform at a time. Izzy hurried behind him, but keeping up was not an option.

He burst through the door on the first floor, the sound echoing in the stairwell. Izzy made it just as the door bounced back. She shoved her way through it and watched as he ran down the hall like he knew exactly where he was going. Thank the gods. Because Izzy was lost.

He turned right and disappeared, but she heard his voice, sharp and loud. "Where is Emma Walsh?"

When Izzy caught up to him, she saw two nurses working on the girl who'd taken Emma to X-ray. She lay in a puddle of blood. Izzy's world began to spin. Michael grabbed her before she could fall and pulled her against him. Held her tight.

"What happened?" he said, glaring at the unconscious nurse.

"We don't know," a radiology technician said. "We just found Camilla like this." He pressed a cloth to the young nurse's head as two others rushed up with a gurney. "You'll have to wait in the—"

"Where is the girl she had with her?" He scanned the area.

The tech finally spared Michael a glance. "She had a patient with her?"

"Our daughter."

Izzy looked up at him in surprise. She knew *why* he was referring to Emma as his daughter. Time was of the essence. They didn't need the medical personnel questioning his involvement. She was just surprised he'd thought of it.

He continued, unfazed. "Five years old. Where is she?" Dragging Izzy with him, he stomped past them and into the radiology area. He spun around. Looked behind every door. Peered through every window.

Nothing.

Nobody.

"Michael," Izzy said, unable to wrap her head around what was happening.

"Search every nook and cranny," he said to one of the lab technicians.

The woman took off, searching every room thoroughly. Izzy's heart beat against her ribs as if trying to escape.

Two officers came up and started asking the nurses questions. Michael strode up to them. There was nothing innocuous about his stance, even with Izzy in his arms.

The tallest of the two turned to him. "Sir, you'll have to wait in the lobby."

"She's our daughter," he lied. Partially. "I want to see the security footage."

"We can't let a civilian see the footage right now. My sergeant is on the way."

He stepped closer to the officer until their noses were almost touching. "This is the girl's mother. We may know who took her. We need to see the footage."

"We don't know that anyone has been taken yet." The officer put his hand on his Taser and stood his ground, even though Michael outweighed him by a good thirty pounds of pure muscle. "I can't do anything without approval."

"You want approval?" Michael asked. "I'll get you approval." He took out his phone with his free hand and scrolled until he found the number he was looking for.

"What are you doing?" Izzy asked.

"Calling for backup." He put the phone on speaker so Izzy could hear, as well as anyone else in the immediate area, including the cops.

A woman picked up. "Special Agent Carson."

"Carson, my name is Michael Cavalcante. I'm a friend of Charley's."

"I know who you are." She had a crisp, firm tone.

"There's been an abduction."

"Anyone…special?"

"Very."

"Where are you?"

"Santa Fe."

"I'm in Algodones. I can be there in forty minutes."

"Twenty would be better."

"Ping me your location. Any cops around?"

He took the phone off speaker and handed it to the officer.

"This is Officer Olivera of the Santa Fe PD." He paused and glanced back at Michael. "Yes, ma'am. My sergeant is on her way. I understand." He handed the phone back to Michael and turned to the medical personnel. "Lock it down."

They complied immediately, locking all the doors in and out of the hospital and making an announcement over the intercom as to why. Missing child. Five years old. Curly, dark hair. Pink hospital gown.

They fitted the nurse with a neck brace and lifted her onto the gurney. Several more medical personnel stood at the end of the hall, peering at the chaos, their faces full of curiosity before Michael caught their attention, and they scrambled off to help with the search.

He had a great glare.

The officer pressed the call button on the mic at his shoulder. "Dispatch, we have a possible abduction. Requesting additional backup. FBI is en route."

"FBI?" the female dispatcher asked.

"Affirmative."

"Copy that. Sending additional units to your location. Do you have a description of the parties involved?"

"Just the child." He repeated the description that had gone out over the intercom. "I'll update as soon as I have more. And I'll get a picture over, too."

"Thank you, Officer."

A picture. Of course. Izzy's cell was still in Emma's room. "I need to get my phone."

"I'll go. You sit down." Michael led her to a cushioned bench and eased her onto it. "Will you be okay here?"

This wasn't happening. This was simply not happening. How? How did Ross find her? Izzy had moved them over a thousand miles away. Changed her name. Dyed her hair, though she eventually went back to her natural color. How had he found her? How did he know about Emma?

"Izzy?" Michael asked.

They wheeled the nurse past her, and the guilt brewing inside her gurgled and bubbled until she thought she might throw up. First Emma, and now the nurse. "Was she stabbed?"

"The nurse?" Michael watched them turn a corner. "Head wound, from the looks of it."

Izzy watched through blurred vision. "I did that to her," she whispered.

"If her life was in danger, she could have run."

"No," Izzy said, shaking her head. "She couldn't have. She would have fought with every cell in her body to stay by Emma's side like I ordered. My ability brings about a kind of blind devotion. Uncontrollable. Irreversible until the target has followed my orders and fulfilled my request completely. Ross, or whoever he sent, would've had no choice but to stop her any way he could."

"Maybe we need to implement that skill once more." He nodded toward the cop.

She turned to him. Michael was right. She had to get into the right state of mind. She filled her lungs slowly, lowered her head, and resigned herself to what she was about to do. "Can you get him over here alone?"

Michael glanced at him and then back at her. "Are you okay to do your thing?"

"I'm always okay to do my thing. It's actually more powerful in times of stress."

"Then I'll get him over here." He stood and walked toward the officer.

He was taking a statement from one of the nurses. "You didn't see anything?"

"No, sir," the woman said. She was short and round and reminded Izzy of an apple in her red scrubs.

"Officer, my fiancée has a question, if you don't mind."

His fiancée. *Our* daughter. Why did every word out of his mouth fit so perfectly? Why did they sound so heavenly? So accurate?

"I'll be right back," the officer said to the nurse. He walked over and knelt in front of Izzy, concern lining his young face as his partner helped the others search for Emma. "How are you holding up?"

She feigned a weak smile. She had to word this carefully. One slip could drive him insane over the next few days. It was a risk she rarely took anymore. In fact, it had been months since she'd last used her ability. Until she got a knock at two in the morning and fell back into old habits.

She checked his name tag, cleared her throat, and gazed into his rich brown irises. "Officer Olivera, you will forget me asking this and what we're about to do as soon as the task is complete."

He didn't question her. He couldn't. He couldn't speak. He couldn't move. He couldn't blink. Not until she finished her orders. "You will show us the surveillance footage immediately. Do you understand?"

"Yes."

"Thank you. That will be all."

The man blinked and shook his head in confusion, then stood and led them to a small security room with several screens. Michael had taken her arm. It comforted her more than she liked.

"Will he remember any of this?" he asked.

"No."

"How is that possible? He'll know he didn't walk to the security room of his own accord, right?"

"The mind is an amazing thing. It will fill in the blanks with the most logical explanations. How often do you think about why you walked from one room to another?"

He shrugged. "Good point."

"Once he fulfills my orders and shows us even a microsecond of footage, his mind will pick up where it left off."

They entered a small room filled with wires and monitors. One security guard sat at a desk, scrolling through footage. "I've been looking," he said, "but so far, no kid in a wheelchair."

"They took her down almost an hour ago."

"Gotcha." He rewound the footage even more, and they watched together until they found a man pushing a wheelchair with a child in it toward a side exit.

"There!" Izzy shouted, pointing at one of the screens. "That's her."

The security guard paused the footage as Michael leaned in. "Is that your ex?"

She leaned in, too. Ran her fingers over the frozen screen, trying to touch her daughter's face. To soothe her. She finally paid attention to the man. Even with the grainy image, she knew it wasn't him. She shook her head. "It's not him. But Ross has to be behind it, right?" She looked at Michael. "He could have sent anyone. He has an army."

"Yeah? Well, my army is bigger."

"Mine is pretty big, too."

They turned to see a woman walk in, her short, dark bob framing a pretty face. She wore a navy business suit as crisp as the winter air and sunglasses.

She took them off and turned to the officer. "I'm Special Agent Carson. My partner is checking out the scene."

They shook hands. "Officer Olivera. We were just going through the surveillance footage."

She nodded and turned to Michael. "Cavalcante," she said, her tone curious. Like they knew each other only by reputation. Recognition didn't flash across either of their faces.

"Carson. Thank you for coming."

"Of course." She turned to Izzy. "You're the mother?"

"Yes."

"I'll need a full description, naturally, and pictures if you have any on you."

"I do. My phone is in the room, though."

Carson leaned closer to the screen. "Is this him?"

"Yes," Michael said. "He took her out the east exit."

The agent turned back to Izzy. "Do you recognize him?"

She shook her head. "This man looks much older."

"Older than who?"

"She's been in a...domestic situation," Michael said. "But that's not her ex." He pointed at the monitor.

"That doesn't mean he didn't set the whole thing up," Carson said.

Izzy agreed. "It has to be him. I just don't know how he found me."

"I'll need a name and the last known address." She turned to the security guard. "Is there any footage of him assaulting the nurse?"

"No, ma'am. There are no cameras in that hall. But we have this of the parking lot."

They watched as the man wheeled Emma out to an old, beat-up Jeep.

"That's it!" Izzy said, pointing again. "That's the vehicle that almost ran me over the other day."

"You've seen this man before?" the agent asked.

"No." She wanted to cry. Why hadn't she paid closer attention? "All I saw was the grill as I was jumping out of the way and then the color of the car as it sped past. I never saw the driver."

The man on the screen lifted Emma out of the wheelchair and put her in the passenger's seat.

"She looks catatonic," Izzy said. "She's such a fighter. Why isn't she trying to get away?"

"That's a lot to ask of a child," Carson said.

Izzy knew that. To expect that of a five-year-old was completely unfair. But this was Emma Walsh they were talking about. She had more gumption than a tween in Sephora. Had the man threatened her? Drugged her? Izzy's vision darkened again. She pressed a hand to her mouth as the vehicle sped off.

"East toward St. Francis," the agent said as she stepped out. "I'll just be a minute."

Michael eased closer to Izzy. She put a hand in the crook of his elbow. He let her.

The agent filled her partner in and came back. "More agents are on the way, as well as several state troopers. How about we get that phone?"

Izzy nodded and followed her out to the elevators, not loosening her grip on Michael's arm. She looked at the families as they walked past, some happy, some tired, some worried.

Her world was crumbling at her feet, but everyone around her was going about their business like nothing had happened. A couple laughed at something shared on a phone call. A child tiptoed to get a drink from a water fountain but couldn't quite reach it. His mother had to lift him. Everyone was just living their lives. No one shattering into a thousand shards of glass.

The agent pushed the button to summon the elevator but stepped away again when she got another call. Five seconds later, she whirled around, her jaw hanging open in astonishment. "We've got her."

Chapter Six

At least once a day, I walk outside and say,
"Computer, end program."
Just in case.
—Meme

When Michael first pulled up to the scene, Izzy saw the fire trucks and smoke and went into full panic mode. She pressed her hands over her mouth as her gaze darted frantically from one bystander to another, her breaths coming in quick, shallow gasps.

Michael watched helplessly as she jumped out of the car before he stopped and ran toward the ambulance. He slammed on the brakes, still several yards from the scene, threw the car in park, and followed Izzy into the thick of it.

A cop tried to stop her, but she ducked past him and forced her way through the throng of people to get to her daughter. They'd been informed she was in the ambulance.

When Michael got to the crime scene tape, the cop standing guard had learned from his mistake. He held up a hand—one he clearly wanted to lose—and shoved Michael back when he got too close. Or, well, he tried.

Michael obliged, stopping just long enough to lie through his teeth. "My daughter is in that ambulance."

"The kid in the hospital gown?"

"Yes. She was abducted. I don't know how she ended up here." *Here* being a house fire on the west side of town. Did Ross start the fire? Had he tried to kill them both in some kind of murder/suicide thing? The mere thought weakened Michael's knees.

Having given the officer enough of his time, he ducked under the tape and looked for Izzy's dark hair. The cop tried to stop him again until he heard a woman's voice. "He's with me, Officer," Carson said at his back. Unlike the agent, Michael had zero concerns about breaking traffic laws to get here. So, naturally, he'd beaten her.

He left Carson to deal with the cop and charged forward. He found Izzy sitting in the ambulance beside Emma, rubbing her back.

Emma sat staring straight ahead.

"Emma, sweetheart, can you hear me?"

She had swipes of blood on her face and hands.

"Emma," Michael said, climbing in to sit across from them. "Are you okay, Squirt?"

Izzy put her ear to Emma's chest. "She seems to be breathing okay."

"That's good."

"Michael?" Emma blinked and gazed up, first at him and then at her mother, as though surprised to see them. "Mommy? What are you doing in an ambulance?"

Izzy laughed through a sob and gently took Emma into her arms. "Sweetheart, what happened? Are you hurt?"

An older officer walked up, his face displaying his experience through the lines and imperfections of aging. "She apparently jumped out of a moving vehicle and ran up to one of the women watching the fire."

"What?" Izzy said, gaping at Emma.

"According to the EMT, that blood isn't hers. Any thoughts on whose it might be?" he asked.

Michael had a good idea. The nurse's. This would traumatize Emma for the rest of her life. Poor thing.

But Izzy was more concerned about how Emma got there. "You jumped?"

Still slightly out of it, she turned to her mother. "Celie told me to open the door and jump when he turned his head, so I did." She looked at the palms of her hands, and a fat tear slid down her cheek. "But I fell and scraped my hands on the rocks."

"Was Celie driving the vehicle?" the officer asked.

"I'll take it from here, Officer," Carson said, coming to the rescue yet again. She flashed her badge, and, unlike in the movies, he didn't seem to care.

He just nodded and walked off to talk to one of the firefighters.

Another agent showed up, a young kid who looked like he'd just graduated with honors from Santa Fe Middle School. Carson sent him to question the woman who'd helped Emma and get a description of the man if she'd seen him.

"So, the fire has nothing to do with Emma's abduction?" Izzy asked Carson.

"From what I've picked up, this fire has been burning for almost two hours. They're just trying to keep it from spreading at this point. It's a total loss. But this amazing young woman," Carson said, beaming at Emma, "used the distraction to make her getaway."

The scraped palms all but forgotten, Emma smiled. "Celie told me to. She said with all the cops around, he wouldn't be able to grab me again. And if he tried, I should scream as loud as I could. But he didn't even try, Mommy. He just stared at me for like ever and then speeded off down the street."

Carson turned to Michael. "Is Celie special, too?"

"Very special. And very old."

"Your *face* is old," Emma said. When everyone gaped at her, she explained. "Oh, that was from Celie. Not me. I don't think your face is that old."

"Okay, then," Carson said, fighting a grin. "How about you fill me in on everything that's happened today while the EMT checks out...your daughter, is it?"

Michael lifted an unapologetic shoulder. "I figured it would get me past the velvet ropes faster."

"That's one way of describing crime scene tape."

He followed Carson a few feet away and spent the next twenty minutes explaining everything—well, almost everything—that had happened that day, including Emma's severe allergic reaction.

"You think it was planned to get them to the hospital?"

"I don't know. Aren't there easier ways to abduct a kid? It seems like a lot of work."

"Do you think he honestly wanted to harm her?"

"I don't know that either. Izzy is convinced her ex is behind this, but he supposedly doesn't even know about Emma."

"Is she his?"

"Yes."

She nodded and took down all the info she could. "I'll need a name and a last known address. I'm worried about the reaction, though, considering how careful Ms. Walsh is. I'll send a team to her apartment."

"We'll meet you there."

Carson tilted her head in question. "Shouldn't you take the kid back to the hospital?"

"I'll see what Iz wants to do." He looked over as Izzy spoke to the woman who took Emma into her arms and brought her to the ambulance on standby. She was shorter than Izzy, rounder, with a bevy of dark curls and enough eyeliner to paint the Astrodome. Izzy threw her arms around the woman, and Michael could see the gratitude on her face as they hugged each other for a very long time.

He eased closer.

"I'm just glad she's okay," the woman said as they returned to the ambulance. "I can't believe she was… I mean, I can't imagine what you were going through. I saw her fall out of that SUV, and then the man just sped away. I thought he'd abandoned her."

"I can't thank you enough for looking after her," Izzy said.

"Me, too," Emma chimed in. "Thanks for looking after me, Mrs. Duarte. Your dad says hi."

The woman chuckled and spoke softly to Izzy. "She must be confusing me with someone else. My dad died over twenty years ago."

"Oh," Emma continued, "and he said to look *under* the box in the closet. Not *in* it."

The woman laughed and turned to go pick up her kids from school. "Early release day," she said as she waved. Then, realization dawned. She stopped and turned back to Emma. "Under the box?"

Emma nodded, a bright smile plastered on her face.

The woman pressed her lips together in thought and walked away.

The other agent ran after her to get her contact info as Emma giggled. "She's going to be so excited when she finds her grandmother's squash blossom. She's been looking for it for months. But wouldn't it be gross now? All squished and rotting under a box in a closet?"

"That's what's under the box?" Izzy asked.

"Yeah. Her dad saw it there." She squinted at the woman's departing back. "She must really like vegetables."

Michael shook his head. Just how gifted was she? He knew several people who could communicate with the departed. Was she one of them? "Emma, can you talk to ghosts?"

She shook her head, the motion sending her curls bouncing around her face. "No, but Celie can. She told me Mrs. Duarte's dad is really nice for an American."

Izzy laughed, the sound breathy like her voice, and climbed into the van again to pull Emma into her arms. "I was so scared, Pumpkin."

"Pickle," Emma corrected.

"I'm so sorry, Precious. I should have been with you."

"It's okay. I'm sorry, too."

Izzy put her at arm's length. "For what?"

"I didn't know what to do when that man took me. Celie told me to be very still and do what he said because he'd hurt that nurse, and there was no telling what he would do to me if I made a fuss. Is she okay? The nurse?"

"She'll be fine," Michael said, reaching inside to smooth a curl over her ear.

Emma stood and jumped from the ambulance into his arms.

"Emma!" Izzy climbed down and offered him an apologetic look.

Suddenly, the floodgates gave way. The fear Emma had been keeping in check came bursting out of her, and she sobbed into the crook of Michael's neck.

"I knew you'd come," Emma said between sorrowful hiccups.

He pulled her tighter, wanting to protect her now more than ever. It was the tears. He was such a sucker for the tears. He'd never make it in the mental health industry. "How did you know I'd come?" he asked, patting her back as Izzy smoothed her hair.

She straightened and patted his face, her eyes swollen and her cheeks wet. "That's why I wasn't scared. Or, well, *that* scared. Celie told me. She said even though she hates you with the fiery passion of a thousand suns, you're still good, and you and your friends would stop at nothing to get me back.

"My friends?"

She hiccupped again and nodded. "She said you have lots of friends with special gifts who can help if you need them to."

This Celie was seriously starting to get under his skin. How much did she know about him and his ragtag family? If she was a demon, he wouldn't let it slide. He would call in reinforcements, which would not end well for the supernatural being. Unless she was into being ripped apart by a departed Rottweiler named Artemis. "It was a very close call, and I was pretty scared, too. Your bravery is what saved the day, Squirt."

She smiled and threw her arms around his neck again. He caught the barest hint of adoration flash across Izzy's face, but for whom? Emma? Michael? The EMT who was still trying to bandage Emma's hands?

Michael glared at the man just in case. He didn't have a lot going for him. He didn't need some nerdy kid stealing Izzy's affection.

The EMT didn't notice. It was probably for the best.

* * * *

An hour later, Michael sat beside Emma's bed as Izzy administered a breathing treatment. She'd also given her another hit of Benadryl, so Emma lay struggling to keep her lids from closing over those beautiful gray irises.

"I've called for backup," he said to Izzy.

Izzy stiffened but pretended not to. "Your friends? Are they coming here?"

"Just a couple. And, yes, they are."

"Are they also members of the Bandits?"

"Former members. One of them was the local chapter's president for quite a while."

The muscles in her jaw contracted as tension built inside her.

"I'm going back to that area to look for the Jeep. He must be hiding out somewhere near there."

"Oh. Okay. I've never had people over. Should I make snacks?"

He chuckled. "They can fend for themselves. And Carson already has a team scouring the kitchen. I don't think you'd get much done in there."

"True."

"Is the girl coming?" Emma asked.

Michael frowned. "What girl?"

"Celie wants to know. She just said *the* girl."

Ah. "No. If she knows what's good for her, Elwyn is in school."

"You're just going to drive around?" Izzy asked, circling back to his admittedly lame plan. "And hope Ross's accomplice was stupid enough to leave his vehicle in the driveway?"

After a quick chuckle, he said, "One can hope."

"That's a terrible plan."

He couldn't argue that. "What's her story?" he asked, gesturing toward the creature in the bed with a nod.

"She thinks she's British," Izzy whispered.

Suddenly wide-awake, Emma's eyes flew open right before she rolled them. "*I'm* not British. Celie is. But don't worry. I'm still in here, too."

"That's good to know."

"Celie calls it cohabitation," she continued. "She lives in a tiny part of me, like the corner of my bedroom."

The thought still disturbed him. He'd seen possession firsthand. He was not a fan.

"It's weird because I have all her memories mixed in with mine. Sometimes, I get them confused."

Adopting a thick British accent, she added, "And she hates it when I's talks like this. It's cocky, you see—"

"Cockney," Izzy corrected.

"—and it drives Celie crazy, it does. Not that I's cares much. I learned it watching the old *Mary Poppins*, I did." She threw her head back, laughing so hard she had to pull her knees up and hold her belly.

Michael and Izzy laughed with her, the sound absolutely precious, especially after everything that had happened today.

"She's so mad," Emma said, her bland American accent back in place.

Michael wiped his eyes and asked, "So, how does one get a walk-in?"

She sobered and flashed him a knowing grin. "Well, one first has to die."

He stilled for the hundredth time that day, horrified yet again by something one of these two had said. He took a moment to let her words soak in, then asked, "How did you die?"

"Eloy Johnson pushed me off the monkey bars. Let's just say I did not stick the landing. An ambulance came and everything. The driver said I didn't have a pulse for two minutes, but then Celie walked in, and I came back to life."

"She brought you back to life?" Michael asked.

"No, silly. That was the ambulance driver. Celie just encouraged me not to go into the light. But that's not even the worst thing that's ever happened to me."

"Seriously?" he asked, a little worried about where this was going.

So was Izzy, if her expression was any indication.

Emma grinned at her and said to Michael, "Mom accidentally tased me once."

"Emma," she scolded softly.

She put a tiny hand to her mouth, leaned closer, and whispered to him, "She'd been drinking wine."

Izzy glared at her. "Emmaline Isadora Walsh, you can't possibly remember that. You were two."

"You tased a two-year-old?" Michael asked, appalled.

"Not on purpose."

"Wait," he said as a thought occurred to him. "Can you use your ability on her?"

She rolled her eyes. "Don't I wish."

"Mommy!"

"Bedtime would be so much easier."

"You don't mean that. You would never."

"Maybe not *never.*"

Emma crossed her arms and jutted her bottom lip.

"Remember Theo Lewis's sixth birthday party?"

"Oh," she said, uncrossing her arms and smoothing the blanket over her belly. "That wasn't my fault."

"What happened at Theo Lewis's sixth birthday party?" Michael asked.

"Mother," Emma said as though in warning. "Don't forget, what happened at Theo Lewis's sixth birthday party stays at Theo Lewis's sixth birthday party. We pinky promised." She held up her pinky as proof.

Michael doubted it would hold up in court.

Izzy dropped her head in shame and offered him an apologetic shrug. "I did pinky promise."

"Can you tell me later?" he stage-whispered. "I'll slip you a five."

"Five dollars to betray my only daughter?" She crinkled her nose and looked up in thought before bouncing back to him. "Make it a ten and you've got a deal."

"Ten it is."

She winked at him.

Emma stared aghast, her mouth forming a tiny O. "The amount of cold, calculated betrayal in this room is astonishing."

Michael snorted. "You have an incredible vocabulary for a five-year-old."

"That's because only part of me is five," she said, pride brightening her face. "The rest is one hundred and sixty-two."

"Well, there is that."

Chapter Seven

List of things ain't nobody got time for.
1. That.
—Meme

It took Emma all of three minutes to fall asleep after her breathing treatment. They'd been worried. She'd just had a severe allergic reaction and an asthma attack and ended up at a fire, of all places. But her coughing had died down, and the hoarseness of her voice had softened.

Izzy tucked the blanket around her and sat back in her chair. "Do you think it's real?"

"What?" he asked, easing back into the chair he'd borrowed from the kitchen.

"Celie."

"Yeah, about that…" He rubbed his chin. "Emma died?"

"She lost consciousness after being pushed off the monkey bars. I just thought the breath had been knocked out of her. By the time I got to her, one of the dads was giving CPR. It was not my finest moment."

"Why is that?" he asked, crossing his arms over his chest.

She peeked from under her lashes and said, "I lost my shit."

He grinned. "Understandable. Were you living here?"

"No. That happened somewhere in Tennessee," she said, thinking back. "We've only been in New Mexico for about a month."

"Yeah, I was wondering about that. How did you end up here? Santa Fe isn't exactly cheap."

"It's not a very exciting story."

"Boring is good." He crossed his arms over his chest and waited.

She looked up in thought, the movement revealing the sultry curve of her neck. Michael had to shift in his chair and look away lest he embarrass himself.

"Two months ago, we were living in a tiny town in Texas when a group of Bandits came into the diner where I worked. It was fine. I just played it off as a coincidence, but they kept watching me and hung around until I had to close up. Needless to say, I got very nervous, even though the fry cook was still there cleaning up. It would've been twelve of them against me and one half-blind fry cook with a porn addiction."

"What did you do?"

She shrugged. "I did what I always do. I ran. Emma was watching movies in the back room, so I picked her up, walked out the back door, and left town without even getting our things from the motel."

"I knew you were smart."

"Do you think so? If you knew what I've put Emma through, you would change your mind."

"Doubt it."

"I've dragged her all over the country. We've slept on streets and in cars and bathroom stalls. We've bathed in park fountains. We've eaten leftovers people offered us."

Michael fought the urge to pull her into his arms. To swear to protect her and Emma at all costs. He couldn't do that to her. He couldn't drag her into his world, no matter his good intentions. "I don't understand," he said. "You could get anything you want with a few words."

She shook her head. "It's not always that simple. I've gotten into trouble more than once. I was arrested in Mississippi for walking out of a restaurant. I'd entranced the server but not the manager. Emma was stuck in a tent outside the city with a woman I barely knew for an entire day. Who knows what that woman could've done." She swallowed a sob, turning away from him to hide her face. "I've learned when to use my ability and when not to. Sometimes, it's simply not worth the risk."

"But you're here now."

She looked around the room, almost in awe. "I still can't believe it. This is the most stability Emma's ever had. An apartment. A car that doesn't break down every couple hundred miles. It's an exhausting way to live, running for one's life."

"Do you know for certain your ex is still after you?"

She nodded. "I got confirmation about a year ago. I was pulled over by a state cop in Arizona for a broken taillight. He told me there was an arrest warrant out for me in North Carolina. Ross had filed charges with one of his cop buddies, saying I'd stolen ten thousand dollars from him. But the warrant had my new name on it. Somehow, he found out what name I'd been going by. I have no idea how."

"Did the cop arrest you?"

"No. I told him the story, and he just let me go. He was very kind. Said his sister was in a similar situation. It didn't end well."

"So, you had to change your name again?"

"Yes. I kept the Walsh but changed my first name to Izzabel."

"Pretty. What's your real name?"

She hesitated.

He raised a brow. "You don't trust me now?"

"I mean, what if all of this is a big ruse? What if he really did send you, and that's just how good you are at your job?"

He sat stunned at first. After everything they'd been through... Then he caught a flash of humor flitting across her face.

"Isadora. Isadora Welch."

"That's beautiful. And it fits."

She ducked her head to hide a smile.

"Speaking of names," he continued, "you didn't happen to catch any of the bikers' handles in Texas, did you?"

She laughed softly. "It's not important. I panicked. I tend to do that." She indicated his swollen temple with a nod.

"I don't know," he said, rubbing it. "I think the Taser was worse."

"Sorry about that."

"Don't be. You're smart, tenacious, and you've managed to keep that girl safe for five years while on the run."

"That's called blind luck."

"That's called being a mom."

She gazed at him with deep appreciation. "I think that's the nicest thing anyone has ever said to me."

He tipped an invisible hat. "And what brought you to Santa Fe again?"

We ended up in the parking lot of a diner on Cerrillos at two in the morning, exhausted, starving, and out of gas. The owner came out, fed us, and let us sleep in his storeroom. The next day, we met his wife. They offered me a job, and the rest is history."

"This apartment is his son's?"

"Yes. And the car belongs to the diner. He had me pick it out and paid cash for it right on the spot. He said he wanted to start doing deliveries, but we haven't implemented that yet, so he's letting me drive it for now."

Michael didn't have the heart to tell her that delivery drivers used their own vehicles. Did the restaurant owner buy her a car outright? "Okay, but why orange?"

"What?"

"The car. It's orange."

"And?"

"Like really orange."

"It's Soultronic Orange."

"Sooo, it's orange."

"No, it's Soultronic Orange." She leaned closer and drew out the syllables. "Sooooultronic."

"What does that even mean?"

"I have no idea. But it sounded cool at the time."

She had him there.

His phone dinged. He checked it. "My friend Donovan is almost here. He also has a Bandits tattoo. In case you're wondering, we aren't in the life anymore. Though we're thinking about starting a new motorcycle club called the Jalapeños."

She snorted. "You're going to name your motorcycle gang—"

"Club."

"—after a chili pepper?"

"Yeah, but it's a really hot one. And, I don't want to brag, but my friends and I are pretty hot."

The look on her face was worth the ridiculousness of his statement. Anything to get her to smile. Or, well, half-smile and half-grimace. Either way.

A soft knock sounded on the door. Special Agent Carson peeked inside. "Can I see you two for a minute?"

Izzy stood and checked Emma's breathing and temperature before kissing her forehead and following Michael out. With Emma's curly hair splayed on the pillow, and her eyes closed, she looked like a doll. Then again, so did her mother. She didn't look real. She looked like an artist's rendition of perfection. Surreal. Striking. Unattainable. Her features were so unusual they could be considered otherworldly.

He stopped short in front of her, and she looked up, paying special attention to his shoulders. "I don't remember a bank vault door here."

"Sorry," he said, holding the door for her.

Carson motioned them into the kitchen. She had brought in a whole team. They were checking Izzy's apartment like it was a bona fide crime scene. Fingerprint analysis. DNA analysis. Threat analysis. Michael had no idea it would become such a big deal, but he was grateful.

Carson pointed to the broken handle from that morning. "I don't know what happened with the oven door, but we took fingerprints just in case."

Izzy choked on air and ended up coughing for several seconds. "No," she said between coughs. "That's been broken for a while. It just falls off every so often."

"Yeah, I keep meaning to fix that," Michael said, toeing it with his boot.

Izzy nodded her confirmation. "He's just been so busy, what with…busy season and all."

Michael elbowed her softly. She coughed again.

"Okay, then." Carson turned and surveyed the forensics team. "They'll need your fingerprints to exclude you from the investigation, but there's a lot going on here."

"A lot?" Izzy asked, her voice an octave higher than usual.

Carson turned back to them. "Would you two like to sit down?"

Damn it. This was going to be worse than he imagined.

"Sit down?" Izzy asked.

Michael led her to the small kitchen table, easing her around an agent taking photos of a boot print. Probably his.

Carson sat, as well. "Ms. Walsh, you said your ex doesn't know anything about your daughter?"

The shrug she offered was born of helplessness, a situation she couldn't fathom. Michael didn't like it. "I didn't think so," she said, her mind racing to figure out what was going on. "I had no idea he'd found me. Us. But none of this seems like something Ross would do. He's just not that…meticulous."

"Meticulous is the right word." Carson pointed to an evidence bag filled with apples. "For starters, your fruit and a couple of other items in your refrigerator have been covered with peanut oil. I take it the strawberry milk is Emma's?"

Izzy nodded and paled before Michael's eyes. Her chest began to rise and fall with quick, shallow gasps. Her dusky irises shimmered with unspent tears.

"Do you have an allergy, as well?"

"No," she said, dumbfounded. She glanced around the room, surely wondering what else he'd tampered with. "Not at all. Why? Why would he do this? Is he trying to kill my daughter?"

"Maybe not," Michael said. "Remember, he had someone waiting at the hospital. Maybe his plan was to abduct her after all."

She looked at him, her gaze filled with realization. "That makes sense. If he found out about her, he would try to use her to control me. It's his MO."

"We've checked most things in the kitchen, but I would throw out anything that can be tampered with. Though it does seem he only targeted perishables. He probably wanted this to happen fairly quickly." Carson looked at Michael. "That means he's been nearby, keeping watch, waiting for his opportunity."

Michael couldn't agree more. "Can you check the cameras in the area?"

"Already on it," Carson said. "But I'll expand the radius. Check convenience stores and the like."

"Thanks." He turned back to Izzy just as a knock sounded at the door.

One of the agents opened it, then held out his arms to block the man's path. But not much could stop Donovan St. James.

"Donny," Michael said, rising to avoid a conflict as the man pushed his way in.

Donovan nodded a greeting to him, then turned his attention back to the young agent.

The kid took a step back, one shoulder raised protectively as if he thought Donovan might hit him.

"He's with me," Michael said hurriedly, showing his palms to the kid. Then he held out a hand to his oldest and dearest friend and dragged him farther inside. "Thanks for coming."

Looking as scruffy as ever, the former president of the New Mexico chapter of the Bandits Motorcycle Club took his hand in a firm shake before his gaze slid to the woman sitting at the kitchen table. Then he turned back.

"Doc," Michael said, taking her hand, as well. "Thank you so much for coming."

"Of course." The gorgeous redhead scanned the plethora of agents that had taken over the small apartment. She had a medical kit slung over her shoulder. "Where is she?"

He pointed. "In the bedroom. This is her mom, Izzy." Michael gestured to her.

Izzy stood to greet them.

"This is Donovan," Michael said.

Though hesitant, Izzy shook his hand, and Michael realized he was wearing a leather Bandits bracelet. She couldn't seem to look away.

"Ms. Walsh," he said to her.

She finally tore her gaze from his wrist. "Izzy, please."

Donovan agreed with a nod.

"This is my fiancée, Dr. Lucia Mirabal."

"Sia," she said, shaking Izzy's trembling hand. "Can I see her? I just want to check her lungs and airway really quick."

"Absolutely." Clearly grateful, Izzy started to lead the way, but Donovan stopped her.

"Can I talk to you both for a minute? And you, too," he said to Carson, who was standing back until all the introductions were made.

"I'll just be a minute," Sia said, patting Izzy's palm. "You guys chat."

Izzy hesitated again. She looked up at Michael. He shot her a smile that he hoped was reassuring and not lecherous. He'd never been great at smiles. Smirks, on the other hand…

"Of course," Izzy said. Trust was not her strong suit, for good reason. "First door on the right."

"Got it." The doc's smile radiated so much warmth, Michael considered turning on the AC. "I'll take good care of her, Izzy."

Izzy offered Sia a bashful, almost embarrassed grin. "Thank you."

They went back to the kitchen table. Izzy sank into a chair as though exhaustion had taken hold. He could hardly blame her. It had been a long day. He could use a whiskey himself. The rest sat at the table, as well—Michael on Izzy's right, Donovan across from her.

Donny stared at her, his expression full of sympathy. Michael had filled him in on as much as he could without betraying her ability. He simply implied that she had one, and that her ex would do anything to get it back. To get *her* back.

"I'm so sorry about what you've gone through today," Donovan began.

"Thank you."

"So, you think your ex is behind this?"

"Yes," she said with a determined nod, a rebellious curl falling over her forehead. "I can't imagine who else would do something like this."

Donovan drew in a deep breath, a soft crease forming between his brows. "I called a good friend of mine from the North Carolina chapter and, I'm sorry, Izzy, but Ross Dunsworth died eight months ago."

Once again, Izzy sat speechless. She pressed the fingertips of one hand to her mouth in thought. Michael imagined her brain was about to explode. He knew his was.

Carson checked her phone. "I just got the report. You're right. Suspicious motorcycle accident, but they couldn't prove any foul play."

"My contact said he'd gotten on the Bandits' bad side." Donovan looked at Michael. "Their *very* bad side."

"Fire or knife?" Michael asked, referring to the removal of his club tats.

"Neither. He ran before it came to that. Went into hiding."

"I guess they found him."

"Can you think of anyone else who would do this to you?" Michael asked Izzy. "Anyone else who knows about your ability?"

Her gaze shot up in surprise, landing first on Donovan and then on Michael with a fleeting pit stop on Carson.

"He didn't tell me anything," Donovan assured her. "He only told me what he had to so we can get to the bottom of this. You have an ability, and there have been people in your life who've used it to their advantage."

Carson agreed. "I only know you're like a lot of people at that compound," she said, her expression full of sympathy. "You're special. You could melt eyeballs with your brain for all I know."

Taken by surprise again, Izzy snorted softly. "That is definitely not my ability."

"That makes me feel much better," the special agent said. No wonder she was such good friends with one half of his employer. The better half: Charley Davidson.

"But there's no one. I learned at a very young age not to advertise my ability. The only other person who knows—who *really* knows—has been locked up for murder in a prison psych hospital for the last eighteen years. And he has a long way to go before he gets out."

"Who is that?" Carson asked.

"My stepfather, Leo Martin Sanders."

The agent typed it into her phone. "Date of birth?"

"March twelfth. I don't know the year. He's in his late fifties."

As Carson took down the details, Michael stood to check on Emma and the doc, but before he could take a single step, the front door slammed open, and a young woman swallowed in bandages walked in holding a scalpel.

Chapter Eight

Adulthood is probably the worst hood I've ever lived in.
—Meme

The agent, treating the living room like his own personal crime scene, tried to stop the woman as Izzy shot to her feet. "It's the nurse!" she squeaked.

The woman looked at her through the eye that wasn't swollen shut. "Is Emma here?"

"Oh, my God," Izzy said. "Of course. I didn't even think of that."

The woman wore a hospital gown and nothing else. Besides the bandages encircling her head, right wrist, and hand—the one holding the scalpel. How did she even get there?

Izzy rushed over to her, but Michael jumped between them, wresting the scalpel out of her hand. She let him, looking at it as though she had no idea she'd been carrying it. Izzy led her inside. The agent threw his arms in the air, giving up. Hopefully, not on life itself.

"She's in here, hon," Izzy said to her. "Let's go find her." She turned to Carson. "She has a severe head wound. Should we call an ambulance?"

"I'll call one now."

"How did she get here?" Donovan asked, appalled.

"In that outfit," Michael added.

The door to Izzy's room was cracked open. Izzy eased inside, followed closely by the nurse and Michael. Doc was sitting on the bed beside Emma, who was still asleep. When she saw the young woman, she stood and questioned Izzy.

"It's all right," Izzy said to her. "She just needs to make sure Emma is okay."

"I see," the doc said. "And how are you?" she asked the nurse, but the woman practically flung herself onto the bed.

Everyone gasped, and Michael pushed past Izzy, but she stopped him with a hand on his arm. "It's all right."

"She had a weapon."

"She can't hurt her even if she wanted to."

The nurse scooped a sleepy Emma into her arms, turned, and handed her to Izzy. "Here she is. I brought her back to you safe and sound."

Michael could see the guilt on Izzy's face when she took Emma from her and replied, "Yes, you did, Camilla. Thank you. That will be all."

The woman beamed at her accomplishment. The bruised left side of her face made her smile lopsided, and her visible eye glistened with tears.

Emma stirred in Izzy's arms. "Mommy?"

Figuring Camilla had accomplished her mission, Michael took Emma out of Izzy's arms and tucked her back into her bed with the doc's help.

Izzy put a hand on the woman's shoulder. "Camilla, I am so sorry. I never would have ordered you to…if I had known. I am so sorry."

Camilla shook her head. "It was my fault. I couldn't stop him."

"No, you tried. I will be forever grateful."

Carson stepped into the room and asked the poor girl, "Do you remember what he looked like?"

Camilla shook her head but kept her attention locked on Michael for some reason, her gaze so intent that he started to feel uncomfortable. "He was older. Sandy hair."

Michael stepped to Izzy's side. "What is this? Why is she here?"

"This is what I was talking about earlier. This is what happens if a target cannot fulfill my orders." She bit down, her small hands curling into fists. "If unable to finish their mission, the target will slowly go insane, and there's nothing I can do about it."

"You can't change your orders?" Donovan asked. He'd snuck in, too, right behind Carson.

She shook her head. "Not once I've given a command. That specific command must be completed. No exceptions." She scrubbed her forehead. "That's why I rarely use my ability. It's simply too dangerous. One wrong word, one wrong syllable, and I can ruin someone's life."

If his fascinated expression was any indication, Donovan seemed to see her in a new light.

A male voice came from the doorway. "What's going on?"

Michael turned to see Eric standing there, watching the scene unfold. "Eric, you made it."

"Of course. Just got in from Idaho. I brought a friend for you guys to meet, but maybe we should hold off on introductions until we can get that woman some medical attention."

"I'm on it," Doc said, walking around the bed to check Camilla's pupils. "We should probably get her back to the hospital. Like now."

The woman started to sway. Michael caught her in his arms and sat her on the bed.

"Will you marry me?" she asked him.

"Not today, love."

Her shoulders slumped in disappointment as Eric chuckled. He turned to Izzy. "Always the ladies' man, that one. I'm Eric."

"I'm Izzy." They shook hands, and he pointed behind her.

Izzy turned, and Michael glimpsed a thin blonde, beautiful with ghostlike features.

"That's Halle," Eric said, the pride on his face unmistakable.

"Nice to meet you," Izzy said. She took the woman's hand. "Izzy."

Michael could tell Izzy's comfort level was reaching an all-time low. So many people, so little space. "How about we go to the living room while we wait?"

"The ambulance is on the way," Carson said. "Is it okay for her to leave now?" she asked Izzy.

"Yes," Izzy said. "Please. We should get her back as soon as possible."

"Can't he drive me?" Camilla asked, pointing to Michael, her fingertip resting on his cheek since he was still crouched in front of her.

He leaned away from her. "Not today, hon. It's Friday, and I have a phobia of driving on Fridays due to a hilarious yet traumatic childhood accident involving a tractor and a pogo stick."

"Oh," she said, her disappointment palpable.

He watched as Izzy hid a grin, but he could see the tension in her shoulders. So many unanswered questions. So much still at stake. They all stood, and Doc began leading the nurse to the living room to wait. Suddenly, a loud, "What the fuck?" stopped them all in their tracks.

"Donny?" Eric asked as he finally took note of him. He gave him several astonished once-overs before asking, "What the hell happened to you?"

Michael glanced from one close friend to the other, seeing nothing unusual. "I don't get it," he said, really not getting it. Donny looked just like Donovan always looked. Though he did seem to have that glow new love invoked. He and the doc had only recently hooked up.

"You—you have no expiration date," Eric continued. "Where did it go?"

Donovan patted his jeans pockets and then the ones on his jacket. "I must've left it in my other pants."

Eric could see the last few seconds of someone's death. He called it their expiration date. But why Donovan's would change had Michael flummoxed. He knew that Sia was something otherworldly, according to the little hellion known as Elwyn Loehr. Had she done something to him? He wouldn't be the first human Michael knew who'd gained some kind of preternatural ability.

"And her," Eric said as though appalled, pointing at Emma, who lay sleeping through everything. "She's already dead."

Izzy gasped so loud that Michael worried her lungs would explode. She lunged forward, rushing to Emma's side.

"Eric," Michael said, his tone anything but gentle.

"No, she died. Like a really long time ago."

Michael welded his teeth together and said through them, "That's her walk-in."

"She takes walk-ins?"

"'Parently. Could you ixnay with the freaking her mother out?"

"Sorry," Eric said to Izzy. "She's fine. Everything is fine. She's not dead. See?" He pointed to the fact that her chest was rising and falling.

Halle reached up and smacked him on the back of the head. A little softer than Michael would have, but they would get along just fine. When Eric gaped at her, she giggled, and he wrapped her in his arms. "We should order food," Eric said.

Donovan chuckled. "Do you ever think of anything else?"

"Your mama," he replied.

"I got it." Michael took out his phone as he strolled out of the bedroom. "What do we want?"

They all exited the room, mumbling about what they were hungry for, and split into two groups. One headed to the kitchen, and the other to the living room that accommodated all of four people. Thankfully, the other agents had packed up and gone home. Only Carson and her twelve-year-old partner remained.

"The ambulance is here," the doctor said. "I'll take her out."

"I'll help." Donovan followed the two women out the door as the doc did her best to keep the back of the girl's gown closed. Poor kid. Izzy had said there were repercussions, but he'd had no idea.

When the nurse turned back and blew him a kiss, he just stood there, unsure how to respond.

Izzy laughed and sat at the kitchen table just as she got a text.

Michael sat beside her, scrolling through his phone as he searched for something they would all agree on for food.

Izzy's phone vibrated two more times.

"Mind telling me what that was about?" Carson said as she sat down.

Michael tilted his head in thought. "You know that whole don't-ask-don't-tell thing you had going with Charley?"

"Okay," she said, changing the subject. "I have three possibilities on the Jeep."

"Way to bury the lead. Wait, Santa Fe has three beat-up, gray Jeep SUVs?"

"Apparently. Farr and I will check them."

"Who's Farr?" Michael asked.

"Really?" the man said, going through Izzy's and Emma's go-bags. He looked at Carson. "I need sustenance first."

"I'll get something ordered." Michael was no five-star chef, but pizza was always a crowd-pleaser.

He nudged Izzy. "Does Emma like pizza?" Her attention was glued to her phone. "Iz?"

She snapped out of it and laughed. "Sorry, what did you ask?"

"Who is that?"

"Who?" she asked, setting her phone face-down on the table a little too nonchalantly.

"The person texting you."

"Oh," she said, laughing out loud. "That was Mr. None of Your Business, Mr. Nosy Britches. He's a close, personal friend. You can call him Nunya for short."

He stared at her for a long moment. "I thought you didn't have any friends."

"Of course, I have friends. Just not any around here. Yet," she added, holding up an index finger. "What did you ask me?"

"Pizza good?"

"Wonderful. Let me ask Emma what kind she wants."

"You don't know already?"

She snorted as she stood. "Have you met my daughter? Her tastes change as often as her name does."

"Ah," he said, studying her intently.

"Be right back."

He nodded as she turned and walked to Emma's bedroom.

"We could split up," Carson suggested to her partner. As they discussed their plans, Donovan and the doctor came back in.

He sat, and the doc went to Emma's room.

Eric was busy making small talk with Halle, so Michael left them alone. He and Donovan had barely decided on how many pizzas to order when the doc came out. "What'd I miss?" she asked, grabbing her purse to check her phone.

"Not much. Did Izzy get Emma's order?"

"Izzy?" she asked.

"Yes." A sharp sense of dread twisted up Michael's spine. "Where is she?"

The doc blinked. She turned a full circle, looking for her. "Wasn't she with you?"

"Damn it." He pushed away from the table and walked to Emma's room and then Izzy's. Nothing. He checked the bathrooms and even a closet or two before realizing the window in Izzy's room was unlatched again.

He closed his eyes. He'd known something was off. She was too jovial. Too sunny.

"What's going on?" Donovan asked.

"I should've known something was up. She got a few texts and morphed right in front of me."

"Good job," Eric said.

"Doc, can you and Halle keep an eye on Emma?"

"Of course," they said simultaneously.

"Did you see who the texts were from?" Carson asked him.

"No. I should've pushed," he said, sprinting out the door.

Donovan and Eric followed him. They checked the parking lot. Her car was gone.

"Son of a bitch," he said.

"She left her phone," Carson called down from an open window. They looked up as she showed it to them. "It was in her room." They hurried back up the stairs and burst through the door, only to have her add, "It's locked."

"Emma," Michael said.

They rushed into Emma's room. It took some coaxing, but Michael managed to stir her awake. "I'm sorry, Squirt, but can you open your mother's phone?"

She rubbed her eyes and yawned, stealing every heart in the room. "Yes."

A synchronized sigh of relief filled the small area. The doc helped her sit as she took the phone, untangled a curl from her lashes with her tiny fingers, and entered her mother's password. She handed it back to Michael.

"Thank you, Emma." He took it, navigated to Izzy's messages, and frowned. "I don't get it."

"Get what?" Emma asked through another yawn.

The doc was busy listening to Emma's chest with a stethoscope. "We might need another breathing treatment soon, sweetheart," she said.

"Okay."

She was such a good kid. But whatever Michael had expected to find in the phone, he found just the opposite. Strange questions, riddles, and possibly a joke? No threats. No dire warnings. Just bland messages. "It's all very cryptic."

"It must mean something," Donovan said, reading over Michael's shoulder.

"What does it say?" Eric asked.

Michael cleared his throat. "The first one just says, *What did the magpie say to the ferret?"*

"Oh, that's Mommy," Emma said.

"What?" Michael scooted closer to her. "What's Mommy?"

"The magpie. That used to be her nickname."

Taken aback, Michael asked, "Do you know who the ferret is?"

She shook her head.

Halle stepped farther into the room. "Ferret could mean a person, but I think they could be using it as a verb." When seven sets of eyes landed on her, she continued. "Think about it. You said she's been in hiding for more than five years, right? Maybe this person is saying they found her. They ferreted her out."

Eric beamed at his friend. She beamed back, only much more bashfully.

"You could be right," Michael said. He looked at Emma. "Do you know why your mommy is nicknamed Magpie?"

She giggled softly. "She told me she used to talk a lot when she was little, so she wasn't allowed to talk at all anymore. Also, in case you haven't noticed, she's a bit of a hoarder."

A hoarder? Michael saw zero evidence of that, so he would just have to take Emma's word for it. "That makes sense, especially considering the second text. *Nothing. Her beak was taped shut."*

"Oh, he used to do that to her," Emma said, brushing a strand of the doc's red hair with a tiny plastic doll brush.

The room went completely silent at her statement, and every gaze shifted from Halle to Emma.

Michael leaned closer, "What do you mean, honey? Who used to do that to her?"

"Her stepfather. He used to tape her mouth shut so she couldn't use her ability on him."

He eased back, shocked to the core at both the news and the nonchalance in which it was delivered. But a five-year-old could hardly be expected to understand how horrible that situation must've been for Izzy. And that explained the small scars on Izzy's face. Miniscule lines that ran from the corners of her mouth. How could he not have seen that?

Growing impatient, Carson took the phone from him and read the next text aloud. "*What is fragile, not like a flower?*"

All three women in the room answered at the same time. "A bomb."

"He put a bomb somewhere?" Carson's partner asked from the hallway.

"Call the office," Carson said. "Fill them in."

He nodded, pulled his phone from his jacket pocket, and walked into the kitchen.

"Okay, next riddle." Carson tapped the screen. "*There is a piggy in the south and a piggy in the west. Let's get the bacon because Daddy needs to rest.*"

"Is there a bank in Santa Fe named Southwest?" Halle asked.

Carson nodded. "The Southwest Bank and Trust."

"They're going to rob it." When Carson gaped at her, she added, "I'm good with cryptic. Piggy bank? South and west? Bacon?"

"As in money," Michael said.

She nodded. "It has to be a bank by that name."

Without another word, almost every individual in the room scrambled for the door, bottlenecking before shaking loose and spilling into the narrow hall.

"I'm staying with Emma," the doc said.

Michael stopped Eric with a hand on his shoulder. "Can you stay and watch Emma for me?"

"You got it."

He patted Eric's back in gratitude, then turned to Halle. "You are officially the smartest person in the room."

She laughed. "Go get your girl."

Michael started toward the stairs but turned back. "Give me one minute," he said to the others, hurrying to Emma's room. "Doc, can I have a few seconds with her?"

The doc stood. "Of course, but she's pretty out of it. Poor kid."

"She's breathing, so it's all good."

The doc left, and he sat beside Emma, marveling at how adorable her curls were. The ridiculous length of her lashes. The pretty bow shape of her mouth. But he wasn't here for Emma.

"Celie," he said, talking softly but loud enough to summon the woman inside the girl.

It didn't take long. "What do you want, demon hunter?" It was Emma's voice, but hoarser and a bit gravelly. Yet it was still her voice, even though it wasn't her talking. Her lids remained shut, hands folded on her chest.

"You've heard of me," he said.

"We all have. You are not welcome in this girl's life."

"Well, sucks to be you, then. If I don't make it back, keep her safe."

She scoffed. "There is no need to waste your breath on such obvious certainties."

"Just sayin'. I would hate to send the daughter of light to evict you, especially after you went to all the trouble of finding such a nice, warm home."

Emma's breathing quickened, and a sheen of sweat formed on her upper lip. She'd clearly heard of his *good friend*. Elwyn's mother, Charley Davidson. Most of those who lived in the veil had. That happens when you are a god known for taking down all manner of supernatural beings—even other gods if the situation called for it. She'd amassed a wicked reputation. Justly earned.

"Relax, intruder," he said. "If you aren't a demon, you have nothing to worry about."

"I am a sentry. A wardress. She had the sight long before I stepped in. I will protect her as much as I am able."

"Then we're on the same page."

Emma opened her eyes and turned to him. "And what happens when we are not, demon hunter?"

"Have you ever heard the term *hasta la vista, baby*?"

She closed her eyes again. "Go. Take care of this threat to my charge."

"Did Izzy tell you anything before she left?"

"She called me old and cranky."

"How old?" he asked.

A smile slid sweetly across Emma's face…because that wasn't creepy at all.

"This is all eerily similar to a movie you may be familiar with called *The Exorcist.*"

Michael could see Emma's eyes roll beneath her closed lids. "In my day, we gave lobotomies to people like you."

"That explains a lot."

"Now, they use therapy and medication."

"Bastards."

"You should consider both."

She wasn't wrong.

He'd hoped Izzy had left him some kind of message. A clue. But it looked like he was wrong. He took the stairs six at a time and stopped short in the parking lot, realizing he didn't have a vehicle.

"You can ride with me," Carson said, pointing to her unmarked black SUV while her partner followed Donovan to his truck.

They tore out of the parking lot just as Michael got a call from Donovan. He put him on speaker.

"Milton is checking the website. He said the bank closed at five."

"Who the hell is Milton?"

"My partner," Carson said.

Michael checked his watch. "It's ten after."

"It's our only clue. We'll start there." She turned on Cerrillos and floored it. "Put out a BOLO for both vehicles, paying special attention to banks."

Michael tossed her a sideways glance. "Your partner's name is Milton?"

"Still on speaker," Donovan said.

"Because that's a great name," he added. "It's got a cool, old-fashioned vibe."

"It's okay," the guy said, his voice filled with sadness. "I know."

Poor kid.

"If you two are finished," Carson broke in, a calculated smirk sliding across her face, "our persons of interest are currently traveling north on Cerrillos."

Michael's head snapped around so fast his neck cracked. Even so, he barely caught the taillights of the Jeep as it passed. "Fuck," he said, for no other reason than, well…fuck.

"Agent Farr, can you look up any banks that may still be open? Focus on the north side of town."

"Did you see her?" Michael asked. "Did she look okay?" He strained his neck to get another glimpse. He rarely got anxious, but he seemed to be swimming in anxiety since meeting Izzy.

Carson pulled a U-turn and followed the gray Jeep at a distance. "I didn't look that closely. I didn't want to tip Sanders off."

They passed Donovan's truck. He had turned into a convenience store and pulled out behind them.

Carson got a message on the monitor attached to her dash. "Okay, I have more info on Sanders." She glanced at Michael, then continued. "Like Izzy said, he was in a psychiatric hospital for the criminally insane for eighteen years for killing his wife. Izzy's mother. He broke out two months ago. He is very unstable and has a history of extreme violence."

"Left," Michael said.

She swerved, took a left at the fork, and offered him another worried glance before adding, "He killed his psychologist after she helped him escape. Apparently, she hired a private detective to find Izzy on his behalf."

Michael worked his jaw, unable to believe the man had managed to find her.

"Oh, and he has an obsessive-compulsive desire to—" She leaned closer to the screen and said, "—to build birdhouses."

Chapter Nine

I don't like people who can't make fun of themselves.
It means more work for me.
—True story

The texts confirmed everything, just like Leo knew they would. Her stepfather was nothing if not clever. Had they released him? Even if they had, they couldn't have informed her, what with her being on the run and all.

When she read his first text, she'd almost blacked out. The world had spun around her as Michael talked about pizza toppings. When he asked about the texts, she'd almost told him. Had almost begged him for help. But how could she do that to him after everything she'd already put him through?

No, this was on her. She would make sure Emma was never used as leverage, and if that meant the ultimate sacrifice, so be it. At least then, Leo would have no need to get involved in Emma's life.

First, she had to ditch the man of her dreams. Then she had to do as Leo asked. If he'd really planted a bomb—it wouldn't be the first time—she had to at least try to find out where. And if she was lucky enough to survive the day, she would do everything in her power to save as many people as she could.

But first, she had a bank to rob.

She snuck into Emma's room and looked around at the blank walls. Where pink wallpaper and stuffed unicorns should be, the room was palpably bare. The kid had never had her own room. This was a first, and it was supposed to be a learning experience for them both. Picking out paint colors and decorations. She'd had so many ideas.

Sia was packing up her medical kit. "She's doing great," the doctor said. "May I use your bathroom?"

"Of course. End of the hall on the right."

"Thanks."

Izzy waited for her to leave, then bent down and kissed Emma's cheek.

"Mommy?" she asked, her lashes fluttering open.

"I'm going to go check on some things, sweetheart. I've asked the Loehrs to watch you if I don't make it back before tonight."

Emma frowned. "Celie says you're lying."

Izzy put a fist on her hip. "Celie is old and cranky."

Emma giggled as she fell back into oblivion, her lids clearly too heavy to stay open any longer.

Izzy pulled her into a hug and kissed every inch of her face. Emma didn't budge. Probably a good thing since Izzy's eyes had filled to the brim with tears. After holding her as long as she dared and rocking her and squeezing her and smelling her hair, she laid Emma back on the bed and tucked the blankets around her.

She would be safe. Her sun and moon and stars would be safe. She would live a happy life if Izzy's boss and his wife had any say in the matter. She'd already made arrangements when the strange events started happening. She knew a storm was coming; she'd just confused a thunderstorm with a hurricane.

Now to ditch the bank vault door. The only way to get out of the apartment without Michael Cavalcante knowing would be to sneak out through her window and take the fire escape to the ground. As fate would have it, that was easier said than done.

She grabbed her purse but left her phone on the dresser for Emma. It had the only pictures she possessed of Izzy and her daughter, all tucked safely in the cloud. Emma deserved to have them. And Izzy knew Michael and his team could use it to track her once he realized she was gone. Admittedly, she didn't know if that would be a good thing or bad. But Izzy had grown up since the last time she'd seen the man who occupied most of her nightmares. Surely, she could handle him now.

The fire escape wasn't quite as user friendly as she'd imagined. After almost falling to her death—twice—and ripping her sweater on the stairs, Izzy finally reached the ground and ran for her car. With her heart trying to beat its way out of her chest, she hurried out of the parking lot and toward the bank address she'd looked up before leaving.

If she got out of this alive, how would she explain a bank robbery?

Maybe Special Agent Carson could help her out. She seemed very at ease with Izzy's ability. They all did. What kind of people had she gotten tangled up with?

And Michael hadn't been wrong. He and his friends were all as hot as a field of jalapeños in a drought.

She shook her head as she turned onto St. Francis. In stressful situations, most people concentrated on the problem at hand. Izzy's mind tended to wander. Like now, when all she could think about was Michael. Would he stay in Emma's life? Would he protect her like he did his charge?

Izzy didn't realize she was crying until a tear dripped from her chin and landed on her hand. She looked at the torn sleeve of her sweater, the yarn frayed at the ends. If she pulled it, would the entire thing unravel? Would she? She felt like that string. Tattered. Ragged. Impossible to mend. She'd been running for so long, the thought of it coming to an end, no matter how bad that end may be, was bizarrely welcome. Her ex was dead. Her stepfather was still insane. As long as Emma was safe, Izzy's world would be rainbows and daisies.

Rainbows. Emma's room definitely needed rainbows.

The sign to the bank appeared sooner than Izzy had hoped. She turned into the parking lot—the empty parking lot—and pulled to a stop, looking around. The bank was closed. Had she misunderstood the text? She didn't have her phone, so she couldn't check, but she was sure he'd sent her to Southwest Bank.

A tiny seed of panic sparked to life inside her chest. She got out and walked to the front door, just in case, only to have her arm nearly wrenched out of its socket. She stumbled into a large bush and realized he had been waiting behind it.

He pointed at a camera and shushed her with an index finger over his mouth. The sight of him weakened her resolve by about ninety-eight percent. What had she been thinking? He was everything she remembered. Sandy hair, only much less of it. Hollow face, only with many more lines. A frame so thin he looked fragile, but Izzy knew he was anything but. He was lanky, strong, and relentless. And he was Izzy's definition of evil. A dry, dusty devil with leathery skin and no concept of fair play.

As she took him in, he did the same with her. His lips parted in a smile that reminded her of a snake's right before it swallowed a mouse.

The second she snapped to her senses, the moment she realized this was her chance, he slapped a hand over her mouth so hard she saw stars and leveled a warning glare at her. Her knees gave way under the weight of it, and she stumbled as he dragged her from behind the bush.

He'd parked his Jeep behind the bank and pushed her in front of him, knowing that if she couldn't make eye contact, she couldn't mesmerize him. She couldn't stop him. He was winning the battle before the war had even begun.

He shoved her into the SUV then went around to the driver's side, never taking his eyes off her. The vehicle smelled like dust and old tobacco. The black seats were so worn, the yellow foam underneath showed through. Empty beer cans and crumpled fast food bags littered the floorboard at her feet. And there, on the middle console, sat a handgun. The kind with a magazine.

It was a test. No way was it loaded. Leo wasn't that stupid, and if Izzy wanted information about the bomb, she had to play along.

When he got in, he offered her that slithering smile again and said loudly, "There's a better piggy up the road. One that's actually open." He started the car and went north on Cerillos. "I can hardly believe it," he said, his grin slicing his gaunt face in half. "If it isn't the magpie. As I live and breathe. Bet you're wondering how I found you, what with the new name and all."

Izzy sat dumbfounded. He was talking like they were old friends who hadn't seen each other in ages and had tons of catching up to do. The congenial mannerisms didn't suit him.

"My psychologist," he practically yelled—the Jeep was loud but not loud enough to warrant the volume of his voice, "hired some private dick. The minute he found you, I knew I had to make my move." He gestured with his hands as he spoke and, every so often, pulled at a strand of what little hair he had left.

She did that to him. She'd given him a directive their last morning together before she went to the police. It was clearly taking its toll.

"I was screwing my psychologist for years." He pretended to elbow her with a chuckle like she was in on some joke. "She liked it that way. Me locked up. Her free as a bird to come and go as she pleased. But in her eyes, I couldn't cheat on her, and that made me safe. Little did she know." He laughed again, what little of his teeth were left making an appearance for the first time. "It was a co-ed hospital, for Christ's sake. How moronic could she be?" He narrowly avoided another car's front end as he changed lanes. The driver honked, but he didn't seem to care.

Izzy was finding his behavior more and more bizarre. Road rage was his favorite kind of rage, but he'd let someone honk at him without the barest hint of a consequence? Maybe the psych ward really had changed him.

"Not that I didn't appreciate the effort she put into our sex life. Know what I mean?" He looked her up and down and glared at her. "Seat belt."

She peeled her hands off the arm rests and put on her belt.

"Anyway, I've had her looking for you for the past two years. Nothing. You were a ghost. Imagine my surprise when my very own Isadora showed up on the news at a convenience store robbery in South Texas. That man could not confess fast enough." He tsked and shook his head. "Always sticking your nose where it doesn't belong. She got your name from the cops and tracked you down from there. That's when I knew it was time to make my big escape."

Izzy had had about enough of his life story. She smirked at him and said, "Don't you have a birdhouse to build?"

"What?" He cupped a hand over his ear to hear her better, then threw his head back in laughter. "Oh, I can't hear you. I'm officially deaf now." The smile that slithered across his face made her shudder. "You can't do jack shit to me if I can't hear you, yeah?" He reached over and grabbed her face as they sat at a stoplight, squeezing until she felt her cut into her cheeks. She fought his hold, but he pushed her away in disgust, slamming her head against the window. "Acid, bitch. Hurt like hell, too, but desperate times."

Acid? He'd *made* himself deaf? With acid? She gaped at him, unable to believe the lengths he would go to.

"Kate did help, though." He pointed to his ear. "My psychologist. She sedated me. Kept me on pain meds for weeks while I healed. Still hurt like a son of a bitch, but at least I finally have something in common with my aunt, God rest her putrid soul. Old biddy never liked me."

Izzy's mother had learned the very basics of sign language from his aunt. That was how they'd met. How he'd become her stepfather. How her mother had died.

Izzy grabbed a napkin off his dashboard as he rambled on about his Deaf aunt, who was a lovely woman. She searched through her purse for a pen and scribbled a question, her hands shaking so much it was almost illegible. It read, *Where is Kate now?*

He leaned closer and squinted to read the note, then shook his head and turned back to the road. "I told her about you, Magpie. My bad. We can't have just anyone knowing about your gift, now, can we? I had to kill her." His brows slid together in thought. "She was surprised when I did it. I was surprised she was surprised. Did she learn nothing from our sessions?"

They took a left at the fork and ended up on Sandoval. She'd explored the charming city of Santa Fe quite extensively and didn't remember any banks this far north. Maybe a small branch?

She wrote another note and waited for the next stoplight to show it to him. *Why did you take Emma?*

"Ah, I thought she might be like you. You know," he said, looking her up and down, "figured she might have that cursed ability of yours. Turns out she's just a normal brat like the rest of them."

A state cop passed them, going in the opposite direction. He tightened his grip on the steering wheel and watched in the rearview as the officer turned off Cerrillos. Izzy got a good look at the SUV's back seat. It was filled with wood and random objects. Things one found on the side of the road. He was still building them. The birdhouses. She'd given him an order that morning, catching him right as he opened his eyes before his brain could adapt to what she was doing. She'd told him to confess to killing her mother, to show the police where he'd buried her body—in the backyard, no less—and to build a million bird houses. She figured it would keep him busy.

He noticed her studying his collection. "I still have to build them. Kate helped me in a lot of ways, but she couldn't even put a dent in that little directive of yours." His anger reared up and he went to grab her hair.

Izzy dodged his attempt and flipped him off. With both hands.

That amused the psychopath. He burst out laughing, slapping his hand on the steering wheel as he drove. "You haven't changed at all, Magpie. Such attitude."

This was getting her nowhere. She needed to know where the bomb was. And if Emma was in danger because of it. She wrote another note, struggling against his erratic driving and the condition of the road. She held it up to him.

"The bomb?" he asked, incredulous. "Where is the bomb?" His jovial attitude did a one-eighty. Like always. He pressed his lips together, his knuckles turning white on the steering wheel. "This is why we can't have nice things. There is an order, Isadora. I get the money, and you get to live." He sat stewing in his anger before adding, "Maybe." He gaped at her as though she'd offended him in some unknown way. "Have you even thought about me? Your only family? Did you wonder how I was doing after that bullshit directive you gave?" He held up a hand to her and turned away. "I can't even with you right now."

Izzy frowned, the expression more wary than disappointed. Leo had always been erratic, but his behavior had gone downhill with age. He was almost childlike in his temperament, but most self-centered people were.

They drove to the outskirts of town where there was little more than sagebrush and tumbleweeds. Izzy had been right. He pulled into a shopping center that just happened to have a small bank branch on one end. But how much could they get away with from this tiny affiliate in the middle of nowhere?

He parked on the side of the building, looked at the gun, and then at her. "Look at you, Isadora Welch. Playing all nice." He fished a magazine out of his front pocket, took the gun, and slid the cartridge inside before chambering a round. "And here I was, worried you'd grown some balls over the years. You're just as pathetic and weak as ever."

He wasn't wrong.

She decided to risk it and see if he remembered any ASL. She asked him with two quick signs, "Bomb, where?"

He scowled at her. "I told you, Magpie, when I get the money, you'll get your bomb." He rapped his knuckles on her forehead, the pain sharp and penetrating.

But it was the strong scent of tobacco that was making her stomach churn. There were too many memories attached to that scent.

"Stay focused, and I might just take you with me on the road." He looked up in thought. "Like a world tour. You and me together like old times, only we are going for bigger fish in the future." He splayed his hands so she could better envision his plan. "Next, we hit a casino."

He elbowed her in excitement before stuffing the gun into his jacket pocket and grabbing her arm. Without warning, he got out of the Jeep, dragging her with him over the console. She had to quickly unclip the seat belt lest she lose a limb.

They stopped just short of the front door. He turned her to face him and put his hands on her shoulders. "Now, remember," he said, far too loudly, "just do your thing. This is a test run, yeah? Let's see how this goes, and we'll decide later if you get to live or not."

She didn't respond. He was delusional if he thought she would travel the country with him, robbing banks. She needed to come up with a plan and fast.

He opened the door, and they walked inside. It had been a long time since Izzy had done something like this. Even her nerves were nervous. The first person she saw was the security guard. He stood chatting with a female loan agent, sitting at a desk on the opposite side of the counters. His uniform didn't fit well at all, and she wore a coat over her…police uniform?

She turned away from them the second she realized the security guard was none other than Agent Carson's partner. How in the…? Her gaze darted to the single teller sitting at the counter. Izzy almost stumbled again when she saw Agent Carson counting money like she'd been born to it.

They must've discovered her disappearance about four seconds after she left. How did they beat her stepfather here? And how did they know where he was headed? She was so stunned, she stumbled when Leo thrust her forward.

He grabbed her quickly so as not to draw attention, then impaled her with a glare. The one that melted her knees and her resolve. Weak and pathetic, indeed.

One more quick scan, and Izzy found Michael sitting at the end of the counter under a sign that read *Customer Service.* He wore a tie and a tweed jacket, the coat so tight she worried it would rip at the seams any second.

He didn't look up at her. He played on a computer, pretending to type something. At least, she hoped he was pretending. He could bring down the whole financial system with one wrong stroke. And where did he get those glasses? Because *day-um.*

But for real, how did they beat her and Leo here, and who'd decided on their roles? Michael would've made a much better security guard than a kid who barely looked old enough to buy alcohol. Then again, maybe that was the point. To put Leo at ease, they'd made the security guard the least threatening individual in the room—including the female cop.

Leo had noticed the security guard, too, of course, but if they did their jobs correctly, the guard would never be alerted to the fact that their transaction was anything but copacetic. That was how they'd gotten away with robbing banks and other institutions for so long.

"Can I help you?" Agent Carson said, tapping a stack of fifties and putting it back in her drawer.

All she did to change her appearance was put her dark hair up and slide on a pair of purple glasses. She was adorable. She still wore her navy suit but had an employee name tag that read: *Bunny.* She was pretty sure that wasn't the agent's real name.

Izzy filled her lungs and released the air slowly before starting. Would Agent Carson know what to do? Would Leo even remember the minutia of the process? Either way, Izzy would have to make it quick.

"Be still," she said softly.

The agent stilled, and her expression went blank. Michael must've told her how to act after seeing Iz mesmerize the nurse. She could only pray she wouldn't blink.

"You will forget us in sixty seconds."

Please, don't blink.

"You will take all the paper money out of your drawer, minus the dye pack, put it in a bank bag, and hand it to me."

Please, don't blink.

"No," Leo whispered in her ear. He'd likely been watching her mouth to make sure she didn't rat him out. "I want more."

She shook her head, refusing, and said the final words that would bring Agent Carson out of the trance but keep her locked on the mission until it was completed. "That will be all."

Leo jammed the gun, still in his pocket, into her back. She sucked air through her teeth but ignored him. Still, the act caught Michael's attention. He looked up as casually as he could, but she caught a spark of anger flash across his face from her periphery. She shook her head quickly, the movement almost imperceptible.

Agent Carson blinked and inhaled as if she'd been holding her breath. She was now in a state of in-between. Limbo. Or she would've been, had Izzy actually mesmerized her. But how did she know not to blink? To hold her breath?

Emma. Of course. Had they called Emma and asked her? Either that, or Michael was way more preceptive than she'd given him credit for.

Agent Carson emptied her drawer, a congenial smile on her face the whole time, leaving a bundle of twenties that surely had the dye pack stashed inside. She zipped the bank bag closed and handed it over. "Is there anything else I can do for you?"

"No, thank you," Izzy said. "Have a good weekend."

"You, too."

They turned to leave just as a city police car pulled up. Was this part of the ruse? Izzy didn't know. She didn't know what to do or how to act.

Leo grabbed her arm and steered her to a door that led to another parking lot in the back, but it was locked, given the bank was about to close. If this had all been real, Leo's panic would've given them away.

"I'll get that door for you," the fake security guard said as the cop walked in. Izzy realized from Michael's expression that the cop was very much *not* a part of the plan. Probably off duty, checking his phone, barely paying attention to anything going on in the bank.

All Leo had to do was let the security guard open the door, but he couldn't hear him. He thought the guard was coming for them, so he did the unthinkable. He pulled his gun.

Michael reacted faster than anyone would've imagined. He was around the counter before Leo could even aim. The movement caught Leo's attention, and he turned, pistol raised and pointed at Michael's chest.

Without thinking, Izzy stepped in front of the gun, and the world slowed around her. Was it shock? The dump of adrenaline coursing through her system? Or just her wild imagination?

Either way, she would very likely die. Isadora Ellen Welch. Izzabel Eleanor Walsh. Whatever name she went by. If she was too slow, she would die. Leo would pull the trigger. Michael would tackle and subdue him. And someone else, probably Carson, would try to stop the bleeding.

As long as Emma was safe. And Michael would make sure she was. Izzy knew that deep in her soul. Knew she could trust him. Loved him for it.

Leo's finger was tightening on the trigger when Izzy captured his gaze with hers. He couldn't hear her, but that didn't mean he couldn't understand her. She signed the word before he even knew what was happening. "Still." Be still. Her opening epitaph.

He stopped instantly. His face went slack as his watery eyes bore into her. The gun was still aimed point-blank at her head, but he stood frozen, unable to squeeze the trigger.

Michael was on him instantly, tackling him to the ground. The gun flew across the floor and stopped right in front of the city cop, who looked up in alarm, hand on his sidearm as he tried to assess the situation.

Leo lay on his back, his arm raised stiffly in the air, tears running down his temples due to his inability to blink. But it was his inability to *breathe* that had Izzy questioning her morals. Her ethics. Her sense of right and wrong. She could let it play out and be done with him. He would never be a threat to Emma again. He would never use Izzy again.

Agent Carson knelt in front of him, and she knew. She looked back at Izzy. "Is he—is he dying?"

Izzy said nothing. She honestly had no idea if he would die or if his bodily functions would take over before that happened. She'd never pushed her ability this far before. Should she let it play out? See what happened?

"Izzy," Michael said to her, his tone soft as he stood beside her, towering over her like an oak. "You don't want this. You don't want his death on your conscience. I promise you."

He would black out soon. It would be out of her hands. And it wasn't like they could convict her for killing him with her super special secret power.

"Damn it," Agent Carson said, starting CPR as her partner called an ambulance. The real employees came out of a back room then, some of them half-dressed, all of them in shock.

"Izzy," Michael said again. "Celie will know."

His words jolted Izzy out of her trance. He was right. Celie would know, therefore Emma would know. But more importantly, *she* would know. Despite her latest nickname, she was not a killer.

She knelt on the other side of Leo and put a hand on Agent Carson's shoulder to stop her. The agent leaned back, already out of breath, and gave her some space.

Izzy reengaged with him, her gaze settling on his, capturing it. She didn't have much time. He would black out soon. "You will forget me from this day forward," she signed. Her movements surprised Michael and Agent Carson, but she would explain later.

Though Leo was catatonic, he seemed to balk at her words. He focused on her as though he knew deep down what she was doing.

"I will not even be a distant memory to you. You will go back to the prison hospital and never try to escape again. You will never hurt anyone again. And as soon as you're finished building one million birdhouses, you will start again, building one million birdhouses, over and over, until the day you die." She leaned closer, signing and speaking the words, "Bomb, where?"

He shook his head and grunted, his face turning a sickly shade of scarlet with the effort. "No. Bomb."

She nodded. "That will be all."

He slammed his lids shut and filled his lungs with air, only to cough it all out and start over again. He repeated this for the next several minutes until an ambulance arrived. Agent Carson handcuffed him to the gurney and rode in the ambulance with him as her partner took everyone's statements.

"How sure are we there isn't a bomb?" Agent Carson asked before leaving.

"Very. He couldn't possibly lie to me in limbo."

That seemed to satisfy her. "Your go-bags are pretty well stocked," she said. "You probably won't need them anymore, but if you do, you might want to add a few Twinkies. They last forever, they're light, and they come in handy in a pinch."

Was that her way of making amends after Izzy had almost let her stepfather die? Of showing her she understood? Either way, Izzy would take it. "Thank you."

The agent let Michael and Izzy leave, as well as Donovan, who'd been in the back protecting the real employees. Donovan drove them to Izzy's car, and Michael took over from there.

They met back at the apartment complex, but before they got out of the car, Michael turned to her, his expression the picture of grave disappointment. "Why the fuck would you jump in front of a gun like that?"

Ruh-roh. Someone was peckish. He probably never got his pizza.

"And we should have dealt with this together, Iz." He looked out the windshield, the barest hint of sorrow flashing across his face. "You should have trusted me."

Her heart fell, despite the fact that her chest had tightened around it. She reached over, placed a hand on his ridiculously handsome face, and turned him back to her. "The fact that I trust you is why I wanted to deal with my stepfather alone."

"That makes zero sense."

"I left Emma with you, knowing she would be looked after. Knowing she would be safe."

"Still a stretch, Killer."

She laughed softly and gazed into the cerulean depths of his irises. The color was too clear, too bright, sparkling in the setting sun. He had shown up out of nowhere, so unexpectedly, and in less than twenty-four hours, he'd shown her the definition of noble and gracious and kind. He'd shown her…

She paused, her jaw going slack as she shook out of her thoughts and gaped at him. "It's Stockholm Syndrome." She covered her mouth with a hand and spoke through her fingers, her words muffled. "I have Stockholm Syndrome."

"I'm pretty sure you don't."

"No, I do." She inched away from him, suddenly wary. "That's why I feel all warm and gooey around you."

"You feel warm and gooey around me?"

"That's why I trust a man I barely know."

"How gooey?"

"It's a syndrome."

"And where exactly is this goo located?"

"A sickness." She pointed at him, her index finger accusing him of everything from shoplifting to genocide. "You just keep your distance, Bucko."

"Bucko?" he asked as she slid out of the vehicle without taking her eyes off him. "What happened to the goo?"

Chapter Ten

I don't always make the wrong decision, but when I do,
it's the wrongiest wrong of all the wrongs that ever wronged.
—Meme

Not many things in Michael's life were certain, but he knew without a doubt that no one had ever called him *Bucko.*

"I guess we'll get going," Donovan said as they stood in Izzy's living room. She had run straight to Emma when they entered, leaving Michael in a cloud of dust. Metaphorically.

"Really? Okay, then." Michael nudged his friend toward the door. It had been a long day, and Michael still had several pertinent questions for Izzabel Walsh. And even a few for himself.

They got to the door before Donovan remembered his better half.

"I'm coming," Doc said, zipping her medical kit closed as she exited Emma's room. As a result, he and Donny were stuck at the door in an awkward kind of no man's land between in and out.

Donovan tilted his head to examine the side of Michael's. "She do that?"

"Yes."

"I like her."

Michael looked at the doc. "I like her, too." When Donovan glared, he added, "Not that much."

"You'll have your hands full, anyway." He gestured toward Izzy with a nod as she followed the doc out.

But Izzy stopped and leaned against the sofa, apparently not wanting to get close to Michael. What with the syndrome and all…

"No, I won't," he said. "No way am I bringing her into our world, Donny. I can't do that to her or her daughter."

Donovan frowned as though trying to figure him out. "You're different."

"You're different, too."

"The fuck?" Eric walked up and looked from one man to the other, astonished. "You're both different. Your timelines are all fucked up. Nobody can screw with timelines like that. Nobody except—"

"The teenage daughter of two gods?" Michael suggested.

Eric lowered his voice as though Elwyn could hear them from afar. "Is she fucking with us?"

"Always," Donovan said. "And often."

"That's messed up."

"Your face is messed up," Michael said, continuing their never-ending game of one-upmanship. And if his calculations were correct, winning.

"Yeah? At least I didn't get hit with a frying pan."

The pretty blonde walked over to them, arms crossed. "Are you boys finished?"

"Boys?" Eric asked. When she raised a brow in question, he caved. "Sorry. Male rivalry took over and caused a robust yet temporary state of insanity."

One corner of her mouth rose. "Just don't let it happen again."

The grin that spread across Eric's face was the most wolfish thing Michael had ever seen, aside from the one he saw on an actual wolf.

"And that's our cue," Eric said. He led Halle out with a hand on the small of her back. "Nice to meet you," he called over his shoulder to Izzy.

"You, too."

The doc stopped beside Donovan. Izzy stepped closer, as well.

"I'm glad tomorrow is Saturday," Doc said to her. "I don't think Emma is going to feel that great for a couple of days. I suggest lots of rest, fluids, and that yellow sponge kids like to watch these days." She looked toward Emma's room and whispered, "Also, just FYI, that woman inside her is cray-cray. She says she's British, but I think she's lying. I get the feeling she is much older."

"Older?" Izzy asked, stunned. "Than Britain?"

The doc shrugged. "I could be wrong."

Donovan peeled the medical kit off her shoulder and led her out. And then there were none.

Michael sank onto Izzy's sofa, a beige thing that had seen better days. "I'll watch her if you want to shower and get ready for bed."

Izzy went to the kitchen and grabbed two beers and two slices of cold pizza. She came back and handed him one of each. A peace offering, maybe? "This has been the longest day of my life, but I don't think I could sleep if you paid me to."

"Are you sure you want to get this close to me? What happened to the Stockholm Syndrome?"

"Ah, Sia checked me out. I'm good."

He chuckled. "I don't think it works like that, but I'll take it." He took a bite, then asked, "I don't mean to pry, but just how close are you to the couple who owns the diner?"

"Because of everything they've done for me?" she asked, taking a swig of beer.

"Yeah, I mean—"

"No, I get it. I was surprised, too, but they are just so wonderful. They've treated me so well, and I let them down. I missed work today."

"I'm sure they'll understand."

"I hope so. There's an unhoused teen, too. I hope she's okay. I try to take her a sandwich or at least some fruit every day."

"So, you feed those experiencing homelessness in your spare time?"

"Just her. I was very much like her when I was young. She camps out near the diner and comes in every day for coffee. Black. 'No frill, just chill,' she says."

Michael stilled.

Izzy didn't notice. "She's such a lovely girl, and she looks really healthy, considering she's been unsheltered for several months. I worry about her, though. A young, beautiful girl like that living on the streets alone? She must be terrified."

He let his lids drift shut as an emotion startlingly similar to blind rage devoured him whole. "What's her name?"

"Elle."

"She wouldn't happen to have long, black hair and huge amber eyes, would she?"

"Like a lion's. Yes. How did you know?"

Michael rubbed his forehead. He was going to kill her.

Izzy checked her watch. "She's probably starving."

"Oh, I think she'll be just fine." Until he got his hands around her neck. He wouldn't kill her quick. He would torture her first. For a very long, very satisfying time. He heard waterboarding was both fun and productive.

A soft knock sounded from the hall.

"You've got to be kidding me," Michael said. He put down his beer and walked to the door, exhaustion taking a very real hold. But when he opened it, his energy seemed to skyrocket. Probably in anticipation of the upcoming torture session. "Speak of the devil's daughter."

"Granddaughter," the girl said, strolling in like she owned the place.

"Elle!" Izzy jumped to her feet.

"Hi, Izzy." At least she had the common sense to look ashamed. As she should be.

Izzy looked from her to Michael. "You two know each other?"

"May I sit down?" she asked.

Michael said, "No," while Izzy said, "Of course."

Izzy looked between the two, confused.

"Is it confession time?" Michael asked.

"Yes." She sank onto an ottoman. She wore her long, dark hair in a ponytail, the absence of bangs accentuating her huge, amber eyes. Even in a hoodie and sweats, the kid was stunning. Michael and the guys had their work cut out for them.

Izzy followed, sitting on the sofa once more but leaning close to the girl.

"I'm sorry, Izzy. I'm not unhoused."

Izzy frowned, trying to put the pieces together.

"The owners of the diner are my parents. Or, well, technically, my grandparents. It's a long story, but they have been raising me with the help of"—she glanced at Michael—"several other people. Including Michael."

"Wait, you're his charge?" When Elwyn nodded, she said, "Okay, but why would you lie about having no home?"

"I'm not finished," she said.

"No," Michael agreed. He sat beside Izzy. "She's just getting started."

Elwyn released a heavy sigh. "I sent Michael to you this morning."

"You what?"

"I faked the phone call about the broken heater and sent him over here."

Izzy didn't know what to say at first. Her gaze bounced between them again before she asked, "Why?"

"It's just...you two are perfect for each other, and it's taking too long for you to get together."

"Tell her the real reason," Michael said, livid with his charge.

"So, you set this whole thing up?" Izzy stood and backed away from them like a rabbit trapped in the nook of a tree by a fox.

"Yes, but not for the reasons you think."

"Then why?"

"There's a war coming."

"Elwyn," Michael said, adopting his stern-uncle voice.

"We could use someone like you on our team. Someone like Emma."

"No," Michael said. "It's too dangerous."

She turned to him and pleaded, "Don't you think she would be safer with us, Michael? Look at her life."

"My life?" Izzy asked, half-offended.

"No," Michael argued.

Elwyn stood.

Michael stood, too, using his height to his advantage. "Her ex is dead, and her stepfather is going back to prison."

"And what happens when the next guy takes advantage of her?" Elwyn yelled, poking him in the chest. "Or the next?"

"She's learned her lesson."

"Michael, you were practically made for her. You're one of the few people in this entire world who would never take advantage of her ability."

"How do you know I have an ability?" Izzy asked.

Elwyn calmed down and faced her. "I have friends in high places." She pointed up. "Very high places."

"What are you?" Emma asked from the hallway.

"Emma." Izzy rushed to her side and put a palm to the girl's forehead. "Are you okay? Did we wake you?"

Emma nodded but couldn't take her eyes off Elwyn. "What's your name?"

Michael picked up Emma and brought her to meet Hell on Wheels incarnate.

"I'm Elwyn, but a lot of people call me Beep." She took Emma's tiny hand in a comical shake.

Emma giggled, her voice thick and sleepy. "I'm Emma, but a lot of people call me Pickle."

Izzy laughed softly, patting her back. "Nobody calls her Pickle."

"But they might if I illegibly change my name. Michael said so."

"Michael said so, huh?"

Elwyn squinted at Emma and leaned closer, and Michael marveled at the reflection in Emma's eyes. It wasn't Elwyn but thousands of stars, as if she was a universe unto herself.

Izzy noticed, too. She glanced at Michael as though to confirm what she was seeing.

"And who is that inside of you?" Elwyn asked.

Emma squinted back, fascinated with what she saw. "That's Celie. She's from England but was in the Americas when she died. The land of reprobates and *ruffans*."

"Do you know what a ruffian is?" Elwyn asked, clearly holding back a laugh.

"Of course. It's like a regular muffin but with more roughage. According to Celie, we Americans *do like our bran*."

Elwyn turned away from her while she fought a grin.

"Apparently, Celie didn't appreciate muffins as much as I do when she was alive," Emma continued. "Or asparagus. She hates asparagus." She crinkled her nose. "I'm kind of with her on that one."

"Well?" Michael asked Elwyn, waiting for the verdict.

"It's a walk-in, all right," she said, fascinated. "I've never seen one before. Not like this."

"So, not a—?"

"No." She shook her head, cutting him off before Emma—or more accurately, Celie—heard his thoughts. "Not that."

Relief washed over him. He'd seen Eric go through what some would call an exorcism. He couldn't imagine Emma going through that. He said softly under his breath, "Guess it's your lucky day, intruder."

"Or yours," Emma said, then giggled—to creep him out, he was certain. She laid her head on his shoulder and was asleep in a matter of seconds.

"Benadryl," Izzy explained.

"I heard. I'm so sorry, Izzy."

"So, a war, huh?"

"No," Michael said. "Not happening."

"Wow." Izzy put an index finger on her chin in thought. "If only I were a real girl and could make my own decisions."

"Izzy," he warned, and Elwyn laughed.

"I have to get home before anyone realizes I snuck out."

"Damn it, Elle." He glowered at her, hoping it would have some effect.

It did. She laughed, gave Izzy a hug, and left.

"Wait!" Michael called out to her. "How did you get here?"

Elwyn giggled and then was gone. Because of her particular form of travel, that meant a departed was nearby. He would never get used to that. There were just some things in life he didn't need to know.

"That kid is going to be the death of me."

"If you'll put Emma to bed, I'll shower first."

"First?" he asked.

"If you want one before you head home, that is."

"I do. Thanks."

She nodded and disappeared into her bedroom.

Michael tucked Emma into bed, then returned to the sofa and his beer. There was something about how Izzy walked to her bedroom, flinging her hair over one shoulder as she looked back at him. The way the light from the kitchen followed her down the hall, only to be chased away by the shadows as they swallowed her whole. The movement created a nostalgic sense of déjà vu. He thought about a girl in a bikini, a brightly colored wrap around her lower half, worn flip-flops slapping against her heels.

He leaned against the sofa, letting his mind drift to a scorching sun and a run-down motel. To the girl he'd left behind. What was her name?

"Your turn."

He opened his eyes to see Izzy standing over him. "That was fast."

"Not really. You were snoring."

"That wasn't a snore. That was evolution." When she smirked at him in doubt as she towel-dried her hair, he explained. "By making that sound in their sleep, my ancestors were warning any wild creatures that they were at the ready for them. Waiting. Wanting them to strike. Practically begging them to. Their survival skills kept the creatures at bay." He stood and looked down at her. "If you think about it, it's more like a growl than a…you're wearing that robe again." He noticed the article of clothing when she tossed her wet hair back and started running her fingers through it. Drops of water penetrated the thin material in the most auspicious of places.

"It's the only one I have," she said, closing it self-consciously.

"Right. Okay, my turn." He stepped into the hall but stopped mid-stride. "Where am I going?"

"Oh, use my bathroom. The one in the hall doesn't have a shower."

Seriously? Another thing he would have to see to during the renovation.

As he stood under the scalding water—at least the water heater worked—he tried not to think. He tried especially hard not to think about that robe and those water droplets and how Izzy's lashes, spiked with wetness, looked like tiny paintbrushes with black ink on them. He tried not to think about her smile or the tiny scars at the corners of her mouth. He tried not to think about the curve of her neck—or any other curves, for that matter. And it all would've been much easier if Izzy hadn't barged in on him, thrown back the shower curtain, and cast him an accusing stare.

Damn it. Was the Stockholm Syndrome back already?

He tried to preserve his modesty—and his manhood—by turning his back to her, but she took his arm and ran her fingers along one of his tattoos. He used his free hand to sweep his hair back so he could look down on her disapprovingly. "Iz, I'm not sure—"

"I've only really been in love once," she said, looking up at him.

"Is that so?"

"For five days. And then he was gone."

"He died?"

"No, he and his mother moved on."

She had changed into a T-shirt that barely reached the tops of her thighs. *Those* thighs. The ones he was trying desperately not to notice.

"I got the feeling they were in some kind of trouble," she continued. "But he didn't really say."

This would get awkward really fast if she didn't leave. He cleared his throat. "How old were you?"

"Nine. No, ten."

Alarmed, he asked, "And how old was he?"

"Twelve."

"Ah, an older man. Do you have anything that doesn't smell like peaches?" He loved the scent on her. Him? Not so much.

"We used to sit at the side of this disgusting half-empty pool and talk for hours."

He turned off the shower and reached over her for a towel. "Did you tell him about your ability?"

"I did, jokingly. I doubt he believed me, but I also knew I'd never see him again."

He dried his face as her words sank in. Her strangely familiar words. He looked at her from behind the towel in disbelief. "I had a very similar experience when I was a kid."

"Yeah?" she asked, gazing up as though seeing him in a new light.

"Beautiful girl." He wrapped the towel around his waist. "Empty pool at a run-down motel in Oklahoma. She wore a bikini and flip-flops. She and her father were on the run, too. I just don't remember it being for bank robbery."

Her smile was part joy and part astonishment. "But that kid's name was GD." She glanced at the tat. Ran her fingers over the initials. "He said it was short for Graveyard Dog. His friends called him that because he lived near a graveyard and, once he bit down, he never let go. He was brave and noble, trying to keep his mother safe, and he had a problem with injustice even then."

Speaking of astonishment… "Izzy, do you know what you're saying?"

"That's why you're immune to my directives. I made you immune before my stepdad and I left."

"You mesmerized me?" he asked, appalled. "Your first love?"

"Only to keep you safe. I didn't know if there were others out there like me. I didn't want you to fall prey to their machinations."

"Wait, you mesmerized me so no one else could?" His head spun with her confession. He remembered her like it was yesterday, yet he could never see her face clearly in his mind. Either way, she'd definitely grown up.

"Have I changed that much?"

"You have boobs now."

"Yeah," she said, dropping her gaze. "That bikini was probably a bit much."

"I liked it." He replaced his wolfish grin with a smile of appreciation. "You were my first love, too."

"You don't have to say that."

"Izzy," he said, lifting her chin. "I've never forgotten you. I think about you so often it's borderline perverted, considering you were ten at the time. But you didn't go by Izzy then."

"No, my stepdad made me change my name. I ended up changing it to something new every week."

"How interesting that your daughter does the same thing."

"Oh, yeah," she said, as though just seeing the connection. "Do you remember what it was when we met?"

"Dora. And now I know why. Isadora Welch."

She laughed, the husky sound scraping his already frayed nerve endings. If she didn't leave, things would get messy. "I haven't gone by that in so long, it doesn't seem real."

"Wait, what made you suddenly remember all of this?"

She beamed up at him. "What Elwyn said about you."

"Okay," he said, showing his palms. "In my defense, I had no idea flu medicine mixed with Patrón would have that effect."

She ignored him. "Your nobility."

"Oh, yeah? I did get an email once that said I was the long-lost son of a Nigerian prince."

She ignored him again. It was probably for the best. "It's so ingrained, you don't even realize how amazing you are."

"I'm apparently a billionaire."

"How unique you are."

"And I have several hundred goats at my disposal."

"How incredible." Her expression almost finished him right then and there. He'd heard of women who could do that. "Of course," she said, walking her fingers up his chest, "there is that one little hiccup in our history."

"Really? We have a hiccup?"

"Just a tiny one. From that time you tried to kill me."

Chapter Eleven

They should invent a Sunday that doesn't have a Monday right after it.
—Fact

Michael didn't remember trying to kill her, but stranger things and all. He shifted the towel, worried he'd embarrass himself.

Apparently, she wasn't too upset about the attempted murder because she reached over and caressed his erection through the cloth. He almost came undone at the unexpected move, her warm touch causing a sharp tightening in his abdomen. He grabbed her hand and held it steady as he gathered himself.

"Are you sorry?" she asked.

"Depends. When did I try to kill you?"

She tsked, clearly disappointed. "You tried to feed me to the zombie gator. Don't you remember?"

"Zombie gator?" He wouldn't have been able to hold back the wickedness in his grin if he'd tried. Which, he didn't. "I don't remember that, but it sounds like something I would do." He pulled her into his arms, mainly to keep her out of trouble. "To get in your pants. Do you believe in love at first sight?"

"Was that before or after I hit you with a frying pan?"

"The first time I fell was when my mom and I pulled up to a run-down motel on the corner of No and Where, Oklahoma, the wind blowing dust circles around us, and there you were, sitting in a bikini at the edge of a pool half-filled with green water, soaking in the vitamin D."

She smiled at the memory. "We used to joke that there was probably an alligator living in there, slowly turning into a zombie gator from all the chemicals and trash." She glanced up at him. "And you kissed me."

He bent his head and brushed his lips across hers, teasing the corners of her mouth where that dimple lay hidden before sliding his tongue along the seam. She opened to him, sending the tip of her tongue out to taste his.

She not only smelled like peaches, she tasted like them, too. He tilted his head and dove deeper inside her mouth as she melted against him, her hand still on his erection. She squeezed, and he pulled her tighter lest he lose control. He was no schoolboy, but it had been a while.

"Wait," she said, pushing him away.

She was right. He needed to chill.

"You said the first time you fell in love."

"What?" he asked, still a bit off-kilter.

"When was the second time?"

He gave an incorrigible grin its freedom to do as it pleased. "I'd like to say it was when this unhinged woman came into the kitchen in a robe thinner than my patience, but that would be a lie."

"It's not that thin."

"It was the minute she opened the door." He kissed the area between her brows. "She wore a paper-thin robe." The tip of her nose. "Her hair stuck out in every direction imaginable." Her chin. "And then there were those damn flip-flops." Her chin. "So, before."

"Before?"

"Before you hit me with the frying pan. Though I think that solidified my feelings."

She shook her head in fascination. "How did we find each other again? How is this even possible? Do you think Elwyn…?"

"Nothing would surprise me where that girl is concerned."

"It would be a shame to waste all her efforts."

"Yes, it would. I just have one more question, Killer."

"Yeah?"

"What was in the cabinet?"

Her brow furrowed as she tried to decipher what he meant. "Cabinet?"

"The one above your stove." He tilted his head in the general direction of her kitchen. "The one you reached over me to get to while wearing that paper-thin robe. The same paper-thin robe that parted just enough to give me a spectacular view of your thighs."

A look of stunned realization froze on her face. He studied her as she thought back to this morning when she came out of her room in a robe and nothing else. In her defense, she believed she'd disabled him. "That's right. I ordered you to close your eyes, but—"

"But I don't take orders from women who are one sandwich short of a picnic."

Her cheeks brightened to a delightful pink. He was probably enjoying her discomfort more than he had a right to. But then his words sank in. She sobered and scowled prettily at him. "Perv."

"Tease."

"So, you don't take orders from women who are one sandwich short of a picnic?"

An electrical current shot through every cell in his body at the sight of her challenging gaze, setting his already fragile sense of gentlemanly decorum on edge—not that he had much in the towel—but he couldn't cave now. He offered her his own challenging gaze. "Not as a rule, no."

One corner of her mouth rose, exposing the dimple he was sure would eventually be the death of him. "I'll bet you ten dollars that you will do exactly what I tell you to do next."

"I don't have my pants right now, but I'm good for it. You're on."

She looked him up and down, her gaze lingering on his mouth, his chest, and then lower, the heat of her stare causing him to far exceed the capacity of her hand before she leaned closer and whispered, "Get rid of the towel."

He couldn't rip it off fast enough—for either of them if her hurried assistance was any indication. She threw the towel on the counter, the T-shirt on the floor, and herself on him. He pulled her tight against him, kissing her like he was dying of thirst, and she was an oasis. He'd never tasted anything so sweet. So sensual. That was when things went south.

She broke off the kiss and glared at him, panting as she did so. "What are you doing?"

"What do you mean?" he asked, confused. Wasn't this consensual? If not, he really needed to work on his social intelligence.

"You're holding back," she said, cupping the base of his cock in her hand and applying just enough pressure to make him wince. In a good way. In a very, *very* good way. "You still think I'm some delicate thing."

"No, I don't," he said, his voice brimming with guilt.

"Remember, Michael Cavalcante. Fragile, yes. But not like a flower."

"Like a bomb," he said, wrapping his hand around her throat and pressing her against the smooth wall. Her words unleashed something primal in him. Something greedy. Giving him permission to do as he pleased was probably not her wisest decision. He kissed her hard, his teeth scraping and bruising her lips as he crushed his mouth to hers.

She whimpered as he parted her legs with his knee and sent his fingers inside her, preparing her for what would come next. She scratched at his buttocks, wanting more. Wanting him.

The shower wall had a small shelf, and her ass fit perfectly there when he propped her up onto it, lifted her leg, and braced one hand against the wall to hold her in position.

"Open your eyes," he said, his voice more animal than human.

She did. She lifted her lids and showed him those gorgeous smoke-tinted irises, like a wild coyote lived inside her. Ate and slept and bred by the grace of her exquisite flesh.

He tightened his hold on her throat and pushed inside. She gasped, her sexy mouth forming a perfect O, but he didn't break eye contact as he slid in and out of her, slowly at first and then faster, pumping into her until the sharp sting of orgasm threatened to explode. But he wasn't finished yet. Not even close. He pushed inside her and stayed, catching his breath, slowing his heart rate.

She clung to him, lured him closer, pressed her clit against his flesh. "More," she whispered in his ear.

He pulled out, turned her to face the wall, and angled her head against his shoulder until he could bend and kiss her again. He held her there with one hand, his tongue assaulting her mouth. With the other, he dipped his fingers in that peach conditioner, spread her ass cheeks apart, and slid a finger inside.

She gasped and sank her nails into his arm, but he held her tight, refusing to give in. After a moment, she relaxed against him. As he massaged, her breaths quickened, grew shallower until a soft moan escaped her.

"Do I proceed?" he asked, his voice hoarse.

"Yes," she said.

"You can say no."

"Yes!" she said again. "Please, yes."

He worked a second finger in gently and then got into position, using his free hand to cup her right breast. Just before he entered her, he pinched the nipple. She cried out and tensed, making his entrance even tighter, but he held still for a long moment, giving her time to adjust. When she was ready, she pressed against him.

He held her with one arm and slid his fingers between her labia with the other, brushing her clit with soft strokes, coaxing her to come. He started slow and shallow, but with each thrust, he went deeper and faster, pounding into her with a ferocity he hadn't felt in a very long time.

Her head was still against his shoulder, and he knew she was close when she whined, the pitch high, the sound expectant. He covered her mouth with his as the whines got louder and pumped into her even harder. Even faster. The sounds. The scents. The sensations. The sensual pleasure of it all caused the orgasm he'd been holding at bay to push its way through his barriers. He exploded inside her, coming in a sea of ragged thrusts and jagged gasps.

She screamed into his mouth, riding the high herself, shivering uncontrollably when she started the descent. She gaped up at him as they stood panting in each other's arms.

"You okay?"

"Very."

Good. He turned on the water, the initial cold stealing their breath.

Izzy laughed and said something to him along the lines of, "Don't drop the soap." He couldn't be sure. He was still reeling.

No matter what happened in the future, he knew one thing for certain. This shower would definitely survive the remodel.

"Are you okay?" she asked as they lay in her bed.

"It's been twenty-four hours."

"Twenty-four hours?" she asked.

"Since we met. Well, again."

She looked at her clock. "You're right. You knocked on my door at two in the morning." She shook her head. "This has been both the worst and the best day of my life."

"I do that," he said. "I've been told I'm polarizing."

She snorted. "You're something."

He pulled her closer, her little spoon fitting perfectly with his. "So let me get this straight."

"Mmm?" she asked, getting sleepy.

"You ordered me not to be mesmerized ever again?"

"To be immune. Yes."

He nodded in understanding. "Did you do that to Emma, as well?"

She looked over her shoulder at him, the grin that swept across her face was more sheepish than proud. "I did. I was worried I would do something I would regret. The sad part is, I did do something I've regretted."

"Really? What?"

"I made her immune," she said with a soft laugh. "Do you know how much easier it would be if I could order her to eat her dinner? To go to sleep? To pick up her toys?"

He chuckled, not believing her for a minute. "You don't mean that."

"I don't. Not even a little. I know what it's like to have one's autonomy taken away. I would never do that to her."

"You're pretty noble, too."

"Really? I never got the email."

"Is this okay?" he asked, referring to their sleeping arrangements. "What will Emma say?"

"I don't know. I've never, you know, had a man over. But I think she'll be ecstatic." She winked at him. "She's quite taken with you."

"I'm quite taken with her, too."

Everything fit. For the first time in Michael's life, all the puzzle pieces fell into place. The odd shapes, the strange corners, they all just fit. He'd never felt so content. So at ease. So able to sleep without a lot of over-the-counter help. Or even under the counter.

Just as his lids drifted shut, she snuggled close against his side. "I use it to ward off evil spirits."

He lifted his lids again, so comfortable and sated he couldn't wrap his head around what she was saying. "Evil spirits?"

She giggled sleepily. "The item in the cabinet."

"Yeah? You come across a lot of those?"

"Not normally, but you never know."

He'd play along. "And what else can this item be used for?"

"Well, historically, it's been used as a form of currency."

"Got it. Evil spirits. Currency. Anything else?"

"I've heard some people use it as a seasoning. Weird, right?"

He grinned, pulled her even closer, and said softly in her ear, "Salt."

* * * *

Also from 1001 Dark Nights and Darynda Jones, discover The Grave Robber, The Graveside Bar and Grill, The Graveyard Shift, The Gravedigger's Son.

Discover 1001 Dark Nights Collection Eleven

DRAGON KISS by Donna Grant
A Dragon Kings Novella

THE WILD CARD by Dylan Allen
A Rivers Wilde Novella

ROCK CHICK REMATCH by Kristen Ashley
A Rock Chick Novella

JUST ONE SUMMER by Carly Phillips
A Dirty Dare Series Novella

HAPPILY EVER MAYBE by Carrie Ann Ryan
A Montgomery Ink Legacy Novella

BLUE MOON by Skye Warren
A Cirque des Moroirs Novella

A VAMPIRE'S MATE by Rebecca Zanetti
A Dark Protectors/Rebels Novella

LOVE HAZARD by Rachel Van Dyken

BRODIE by Aurora Rose Reynolds
An Until Her Novella

THE BODYGUARD AND THE BOMBSHELL by Lexi Blake
A Masters and Mercenaries: New Recruits Novella

THE SUBSTITUTE by Kristen Proby
A Single in Seattle Novella

CRAVED BY YOU by J. Kenner
A Stark Security Novella

GRAVEYARD DOG by Darynda Jones
A Charley Davidson Novella

A CHRISTMAS AUCTION by Audrey Carlan
A Marriage Auction Novella

THE GHOST OF A CHANCE by Heather Graham
A Krewe of Hunters Novella

Also from Blue Box Press

LEGACY OF TEMPTATION by Larissa Ione
A Demonica Birthright Novel

VISIONS OF FLESH AND BLOOD by Jennifer L. Armentrout and Ravyn Salvador
A Blood & Ash and Fire & Flesh Compendium

FORGETTING TO REMEMBER by M.J. Rose

TOUCH ME by J. Kenner
A Stark International Novella

BORN OF BLOOD AND ASH by Jennifer L. Armentrout
A Flesh and Fire Novel

MY ROYAL SHOWMANCE by Lexi Blake
A Park Avenue Promise Novel

SAPPHIRE DAWN by Christopher Rice writing as C. Travis Rice
A Sapphire Cove Novel

EMBRACING THE CHANGE by Kristen Ashley
A River Rain Novel

IN THE AIR TONIGHT by Marie Force

LEGACY OF CHAOS by Larissa Ione
A Demonica Birthright Novel

Discover Darynda Jones

The Grave Robber
A Charley Davidson Novella

Eric Vause is done.

Done with ghosts. Done with hellhounds. And definitely done with asshole demons, mostly because he'd been possessed by one. Even now, five years later, the rage he absorbed from the creature has yet to wane, so he decides a road trip is in order. Surely some cool air, great scenery, and a case of Dos Equis will shake things loose. Unfortunately, supernatural events happen everywhere. When he meets up with a friend whose partner's daughter needs help with a pest problem—aka, a ghost—Eric takes that as his cue to leave.

Until he sees her.

He can tell Halle's house isn't the only thing that is haunted. The hopelessness behind her eyes tugs at something deep inside him. Something all too familiar. The fact that she's the most beautiful woman he's ever seen has nothing to do with his change of heart. And he vows to leave her in his rearview the minute he takes care of the poltergeist. Then again, vows were never his strong suit.

* * * *

The Graveside Bar and Grill
A Charley Davidson Novella

When Donovan St. James' precocious charge asks him—no questions asked—to tail the doctor who keeps their ragtag team patched up, he wants to refuse. Not because the saucy teen is getting too big for her britches, ordering him around like a mob boss, but because the woman stirs feelings in him he would rather not explore. However, when evil threatens the doc's life, he realizes he has no choice. Sia saved his life once. He will try to return the favor. He just prays he can do it without losing his heart.

Running from the supernatural entity that has destroyed entire worlds to have her, Sia thought she'd found a haven on Earth with a motley team of warriors protecting the girl destined to save humanity. But when Sia's found, she realizes something on this plane is more scrumptious than her: that very teen. So, she runs—and Donovan St. James follows. Nothing is more alluring than a scruffy biker with a lacerating gaze. And she vows to tell him that…if they survive.

* * * *

The Gravedigger's Son
A Charley Davidson Novella

The job should have been easy.

Get in. Assess the situation. Get out. But for veteran tracker Quentin Rutherford, things get sticky when the girl he's loved since puberty shows up, conducting her own investigation into the strange occurrences of the small, New Mexico town. He knew it would be a risk coming back to the area, but he had no idea Amber Kowalski had become a bona fide PI, investigating things that go bump in the night. He shouldn't be surprised, however. She can see through the dead as clearly as he can. The real question is, can she see through him?

But is anything that's worth it ever easy?

To say that Amber is shocked to see her childhood crush would be the understatement of her fragile second life. One look at him tells her everything she needs to know. He's changed. So drastically she barely recognizes him. He is savage now, a hardened—in all the right places—demon hunter, and she is simply the awkward, lovestruck girl he left behind.

But she doesn't have time to dwell on the past. A supernatural entity has set up shop, and it's up to them to stop it before it kills again.

While thousands of questions burn inside her, she has to put her concern over him, over what he's become, aside for now. Because he's about to learn one, undeniable fact: she's changed, too.

* * * *

The Graveyard Shift
A Charley Davidson Novella

Guarding a precocious five-year-old who is half-human, half-god, and 100% destined to save the world is no easy feat.

Garrett Swopes was the ultimate skeptic until he met a certain hellion and her husband. They vanished after stopping a catastrophic event and left him, a mere mortal, in charge of protecting their gift to mankind. But when she disappears as well, he needs the help of another breed of hellion. One who can see past the veil of space and time. One who betrayed him.

She will get a truce in the deal, but she will never earn his forgiveness.

Marika Dubois's son—a warrior in the coming war between heaven and hell—was foreseen long before his birth. But to create a child strong enough to endure the trials that lay ahead, she needed a descendant of powerful magics. She found that in Garrett Swopes and tricked him into fathering her son. A ploy he has never forgiven her for. But when he knocks on her door asking for her help, she sees the fierce attraction he tries to deny rise within him.

And Marika has to decide if she dares risk her heart a second time to help the only man she's ever loved.

An excerpt from
The Grave Robber
by Darynda Jones

Eric Vause is done.

Done with ghosts. Done with hellhounds. And definitely done with asshole demons, mostly because he'd been possessed by one. Even now, five years later, the rage he absorbed from the creature has yet to wane, so he decides a road trip is in order. Surely some cool air, great scenery, and a case of Dos Equis will shake things loose. Unfortunately, supernatural events happen everywhere. When he meets up with a friend whose partner's daughter needs help with a pest problem—aka, a ghost—Eric takes that as his cue to leave.

Until he sees her.

He can tell Halle's house isn't the only thing that is haunted. The hopelessness behind her eyes tugs at something deep inside him. Something all too familiar. The fact that she's the most beautiful woman he's ever seen has nothing to do with his change of heart. And he vows to leave her in his rearview the minute he takes care of the poltergeist. Then again, vows were never his strong suit.

* * * *

"My dad told me about you. Jason has him convinced you're the real deal."

"The real deal?"

"That you can see into the supernatural world."

"Oh!" Aunt Lil said, squirming in a chair that just happened to be pulled out enough for her to pretend to squeeze into it. "Tell her about me!"

"Jason's a pathological liar."

A dimple appeared at one corner of her mouth. Amazing how something so small could shake me so hard. "I've heard that about him." She wrapped both hands around the mug and took a sip of tea as though bracing herself for her next words. "You helped me," she said after swallowing hard. "At the gas station, you helped me get that pump, even after I treated you so horrendously. Why?"

"I'm a member of the Knights in Shining Armor Club. It's mandatory that we help one maiden in distress a day or we lose our parking privileges."

She pursed her lips, trying to keep a wayward grin at bay. "You don't say."

"We also get a ten-percent discount at Cracker Barrel."

This time, she laughed—a beautiful, lyrical sound that…

Holy fuck, I had to stop. This was getting ridiculous. I needed to get out of here before I dropped to one knee and proposed. I scanned the bar. Wasn't there a redhead around here somewhere? Someone, anyone to take my mind off Halle Nordstrom.

"Do you really have experience with all that stuff?"

I refocused on her and absently lifted a shoulder. "There are few people on the planet with more." Besides some of my closest friends, but that was a story for another day.

The heat from Aunt Lil's glare almost seared the flesh off my face. "You're not going to tell her about me, are you?"

"Jason says you can even see when people are going to die."

I rolled my eyes. Did that asshole spill all my secrets?

"You're ashamed of me, aren't you?" Aunt Lil pouted, crossing her arms over her muumuu-clad chest.

"So, what?" Halle asked with a soft laugh to lighten her next question. "You're like…the grim reaper?"

"No, but she's a good friend of mine."

Her mouth formed a hesitant grin. "You say the funniest things."

"Well, I'm also a member of the National Association for the Fair and Ethical Treatment of Stand-up Comedians, so…"

I saw she wanted to laugh but couldn't quite manage it. Her next question seemed to weigh too heavily on her mind. She stuck a chewed fingernail between her teeth and asked softly, "Can you see when I'm going to die?"

I shook my head. "Sorry."

"And now you're lying to her." Aunt Lil tsked at me.

"It comes and goes," I added, lying my ass off.

"Ah." Relief softened the convex curve of Halle's shoulders, a reaction I didn't expect. But, of course, she would be relieved. She didn't want me to throw a wrench into her final plans.

But again, none of this was my problem. I only helped those in immediate danger, and even then, it had to be a life-or-death situation. Something I couldn't fuck up too badly. Halle may very well be haunted, though I still had my doubts, but I could hardly do anything about it either way. Her impending doom could be thwarted with good timing and a little luck, so my job here was done. Now, to leave. Get up and say my goodbyes. How hard could it be?

"Are you really going to ignore me all night, Constantine?"

Why did Aunt Lil love my middle name so much? I started to cast her a quick scowl to shush her—not that my threats ever worked—but changed my mind. Maybe she was my ticket out of this situation. My escape. Perhaps I didn't have to leave after all and look like an asshole—not that I wasn't. I just needed to scare Halle off so she did the leaving.

I pulled my mouth into a calculated smile, turned, and looked straight at Aunt Lil. "Did your niece send you to watch over me?"

Aunt Lil stared at me, her lids fluttering in confusion. "My niece?"

"You remember her. Charley Davidson? The saucy one with brown hair and a killer dropkick?"

She came to her senses and crossed her arms over her love beads. "So, we're on speaking terms again?"

"What are you doing?" Halle asked, her expression wary.

About Darynda Jones

NY Times and *USA Today* Bestselling Author Darynda Jones has won numerous awards for her work and her books have been translated into 17 languages. As a born storyteller, Darynda grew up spinning tales of dashing damsels and heroes in distress for any unfortunate soul who happened by, certain they went away the better for it. She penned the internationally bestselling Charley Davidson series and is currently working on several beloved projects, most notably the Sunshine Vicram Mystery Series with St. Martin's Press and the Betwixt and Between Series of paranormal women's fiction. She lives in the Land of Enchantment, also known as New Mexico, with her husband and two beautiful sons, the Mighty, Mighty Jones Boys.

She can be found at http://www.daryndajones.com

On Behalf of 1001 Dark Nights,

Liz Berry, M.J. Rose, and Jillian Stein would like to thank ~

Steve Berry
Doug Scofield
Benjamin Stein
Kim Guidroz
Chelle Olson
Tanaka Kangara
Asha Hossain
Chris Graham
Suzy Baldwin
Jessica Saunders
Stacey Tardif
Grace Wenk
Dylan Stockton
Kate Boggs
Richard Blake
and Simon Lipskar

Made in United States
Troutdale, OR
11/19/2024